The Adventurers
Ordinary people with special callings

by
Diane Forrest

**Wood Lake Books
and
The Upper Room**

Design by Jim Taylor

Illustrations by Phil Clark, Penticton, B.C.

Published co-operatively by:

Wood Lake Books, Inc.,
Box 700,
Winfield, BC, V0H 2C0
Canada

The Upper Room
1908 Grand Ave., Box 189
Nashville, TN, 37202-0189
U.S.A.

Canadian Cataloguing in Publication Data

Forrest, Diane, 1955-
     The adventurers

Canadian ISBN 0-919599-10-9   U.S.A. ISBN 0-8358-0497-6

   1. Christian biography - Juvenile
literature. I. Title.
BR1704.F67   j280'.092'2   c83-091225-8

Printed in Canada by

Friesen Printers

Altona, Manitoba

R0G 0B0

To
the children and young people
of
St. Andrew's United Church

CONTENTS

ACKNOWLEDGEMENTS

Most of the information in *The Adventurers* came from secondary sources. I have tried as much as possible to base the dialogue on recorded conversations; in some cases, however, I have simplified the language.

A number of people kindly consented to be interviewed for this book: Florence Hall (formerly Florence Liddell), David Michell, Bob McClure and Nancy Hudson (who worked with Mother Teresa) were all generous with their time and memories. Thanks are also due to the St. Andrew's United Church confirmation class of 1982-83, who were both my inspiration and my kindest critics, and to my fellow teachers in that class, Dr. Richard Davidson and Lynne Elder.

My family and friends gave much needed support, always asking the right questions at the right times. Christine McClymont made valuable suggestions based on her experience as an educational writer and editor, while my sister Susan Forrest applied the expertise of the classroom to the manuscript.

Lastly, I thank Jim Taylor and Ralph Milton of Wood Lake Books, for giving me what seemed the unbelievable opportunity to write this book, and Ken Bagnell, editor of *The Review*, who gave me the training that made the writing possible.

INTRODUCTION

Christmas is a bad time to be a Sunday School teacher.

Once again I was out looking for Christmas books to give to the kids in my Sunday School class. As usual, I couldn't find anything I was sure would be good. I knew they'd already read the *Narnia* books, *The Cross and the Switchblade* and *The Hiding Place*. The books I'd enjoyed at their age seemed to be out of print.

That's when the idea came. If I didn't like what was available, why didn't I write something myself? I talked about *The Adventurers* to Jim Taylor, a friend who had recently started a publishing company, and he encouraged me to start writing.

The people I've written about in this book were chosen arbitrarily; they happen to be people I am interested in. But they all have in common the fact that they were willing to risk their careers, their friendships and family ties, and even their lives because they believed there was something God wanted them to do. They all proved dramatically that being a Christian is an adventure.

You may not agree with what all of them did. And if you read more about them, you will find that they all had flaws, that they were all men and women of their own time and place, with beliefs that we may sometimes find odd or objectionable. But that only makes the success of their adventures more remarkable.

I have enjoyed writing this book. I hope you will enjoy reading it, whatever your age.

Diane Forrest

ST. FRANCIS

The madman of Assisi

ST. FRANCIS OF ASSISI

The winter of 1207 was the coldest anyone could remember. But despite the weather, the piazza in the little Italian city of Assisi was packed. Nobody would have missed Bishop Guido's court that morning.

The crowd buzzed with story after story about Francis Bernardone, the defendant in the case.

For a while, he had been the most popular young man in town, arranging banquets and dances and concerts for the young nobles. Though Francis was only a cloth merchant's son, the nobles were happy to have him—especially when he paid all the bills.

One old woman shook her head. Francis used to be a brave, good-hearted boy, but he'd never recovered from a fever he had caught. He came back from the war saying God had spoken to him. After that he took to wandering around the hills of Assisi.

He claimed that Christ had spoken to him at the crumbling old church of San Damiano, telling him to rebuild his church. Francis immediately took the finest bolts of silk and velvet from his father's shop and sold them to buy construction materials. The man telling that story almost choked with laughter. It served old Pietro Bernardone right. Francis' father had been so proud of his spendthrift son, so sure he'd bring glory to the family. In his fury Pietro chained Francis in the cellar, but his mother set him free.

Now Francis had agreed to let the bishop decide the case. In a magnificent blue velvet cloak, surrounded by his officials, Assisi's bishop gestured to the merchant to tell his story. Pietro argued forcefully—Francis had robbed him and embarassed the whole family by his strange behaviour. He should be banished from the city.

The crowd began to mutter. In Italy in the Middle Ages, banishment could ruin a man's life, cutting him off from his family and friends and following him like a curse everywhere he went.

Bishop Guido frowned and turned to the slight figure dressed in rags, thin from missed meals, hard work and long nights of prayer. Was this the young man who had been the troubadour of Assisi, who had sat up at night designing ever more gorgeous clothing to amaze his friends, who had dreamed of becoming a great knight?

"Francis," said the bishop, "you have disturbed and shocked your father. It is good that you want to serve God, but you can't do it with other people's money. Give him back his gold, and everyone will be satisfied."

The young man hesitated for a moment, frowning. Perhaps Bishop Guido was right. But would he ever be free of this constant wrangling about money and property?

"Very well, Lord Bishop," he said. "I will return everything to my father."

He ran into the bishop's palace. A moment later he was back, carrying not only the gold he had earned from selling the cloth but all of his clothes.

Naked in the cold, except for a loincloth, he approached Pietro. "Father, I give everything back to you. From now on I will serve only God."

Then he turned to the crowd. "Up until today I have called Pietro Bernardone my father. For the future I will say, 'Our Father, who art in heaven... .'"

Pietro took the money and clothes, gaping at his son.

The bishop too was stunned. Francis was turning his back on everything that counted in this world—his family, his profession, his friends, his old dreams. Was he insane? But something stirred in the back of the bishop's mind: "If anyone comes to me and cannot turn his back on his father and mother and wife and children and brothers and sisters, yes, and even his own life, he cannot be my disciple." Rising from his throne, his gold hat glinting in the sunlight, the bishop walked over to the shivering young man and placed his velvet robe about Francis' frail shoulders.

The people of Assisi soon became accustomed to the sight of Francis in ragged clothes standing on the street corners, asking for money and building materials to restore the church of San Damiano. Some gave him money. Others jeered and spat at him.

Francis only replied, "The Lord give you peace."

Francis knew his behaviour seemed crazy to other people, but he had to keep searching to find out what God wanted him to do. All his life he had been looking for the right way to live. He had tried to be a successful merchant, like his father, but he couldn't see the point of piling up more and more money. He had wanted to be a great knight, fighting bravely, helping the weak, winning the love of a great lady. But he knew now that war was cruel and brutal.

In fact, life everywhere seemed to be cruel. Nobles despised business people. Business people were only interested in making money. Serfs lived in poverty and were forced to serve others.

Francis looked to the Church for guidance, but it too seemed corrupt. Many of the clergy lived in luxury, amassing huge fortunes while ignoring their vows of poverty. Some demanded payment when they forgave people for their sins. Even honest bishops like Guido were forever fighting with the authorities to get more money and power for the Church, because they believed that God wanted the Church to have political as well as spiritual power.

Francis thought about Jesus. He hadn't advised people to seek wealth and power. In fact, sometimes Jesus seemed to say that it was better to be poor. And as he wandered over the rich green hills above the city, seeing the grandeur of the crags, smelling the spring flowers on the wind, hearing the call of the skylark, Francis wondered why people needed so many things when God had already given them so much.

One day in the streets of Assisi, Francis saw an old friend, one of the nobles from his carousing days. But Bernard had always been more serious than the others. Now he was curious about his friend's strange behaviour. "Will you dine with me this evening, Francis?" he asked.

Over the splendid dinner, over the silver and fine plates, Francis told Bernard what he had been thinking. "All of these things are delightful," he said, waving his hand at the sumptuously laid table. "But often we become so absorbed in them that we forget the important things in life, even our duty to God."

Bernard agreed. But how could they best serve God? The next morning they went to a nearby church, where Francis asked the priest to open the Gospels three times and read the passages he found.

The first read: "If you seek perfection, go, sell your possessions and give to the poor. You will then have treasure in heaven."

The next was from Christ's instructions to his disciples: "Take nothing on the way."

The third passage was, "If a man wishes to come after me, he must deny his very self."

They had their answer.

Bernard immediately went and sold his property, giving everything he had to the poor. Then he and Francis retired to a little church in the hills above Assisi, called the Portiuncula, where they built shacks to live in.

People in Assisi began to wonder if Francis Bernardone's madness was catching, for more men were going to the Portiuncula. Soon he had 12 disciples.

The men decided to call themselves the Friars Minor, to indicate that they did not want any power or glory for themselves. Together they planned to live their lives the way that Jesus had lived his: wandering through the countryside preaching, praying, living a simple life, owning nothing and relying on God to provide for them. Not that they were afraid of work. They took jobs helping in the fields or in the leprosy hospitals, for which they received only food and clothing, since they were not to have any money. They tried to treat everyone courteously, putting other people's needs before their own.

Yet though the brothers' lives seemed hard and solemn, the forest around the Portiuncula rang with laughter and song. Now that they didn't have to worry about making money or impressing other people, Francis and his brothers found that they were enjoying life much more. Francis had no use for so-called men of God who always looked glum. "How can we be sad when God has given us so much?" he would ask his friends.

As the little group at the Portiuncula grew, Francis realized that there might be a different interpretation to the message he had received at San Damiano. Perhaps Christ did not want him to restore actual churches but to help restore the Church itself to virtue. If his work was to continue to grow, then he must seek the approval of the pope.

Bernard organized the trip. Singing their hymns of praise along the way, the brothers set out for Rome. When they arrived, they were surprised to find that Bishop Guido was already there.

Ever since that day in the piazza, Bishop Guido had been encouraging Francis, even though the crafty clergyman and *Il Poverello,* "the little poor man," were very different. Now Guido introduced Francis and his brothers to an influential cardinal.

There would be many difficulties in having their plan to found a new order approved, the cardinal warned. Many men had started out, as they had, by seeking to live a simple life and had ended up opposing the church and siding with its enemies. But Francis was determined. Cardinal John, impressed by the sincerity of his guests and their loyalty to the Church, agreed to support them.

A few days later Francis and his companions found themselves kneeling on the richly coloured mosaic of the pope's audience room, their ragged brown habits stark against the rich crimson of the cardinals' robes and the gold-embroidered mantle of the pope himself. Quietly and slowly Francis explained that the brothers simply wanted to live exactly the way Jesus had lived. The pope tried to be polite, but he was getting tired of fanatics. He suggested they pray about it and meet again tomorrow.

Cardinal John and Bishop Guido shook their heads in discouragement.

That night the pope had a dream. He was standing in the great church of St. John Lateran, the head church of the Catholic faith. Suddenly the whole building began to shake and crumble. As the stones began to fall, a man ran up and supported the building. The shaking stopped. The church was whole again. The pope awoke with a start. That figure had seemed very familiar, with its ragged habit....

The next day, the cardinals argued. It was impossible for anyone to follow such a hard life, most of them said. Then Cardinal John stood up. "This man is only asking to be allowed to live according to the Gospels," he said. "If we say that that is impossible, then we are saying that the Gospels and therefore Jesus Christ are wrong."

The pope chuckled to himself. The Cardinal had them cornered. He motioned to the figure standing in the shadows. "And what do you say to this, little brother?"

"Your Holiness, this reminds me of the story of the great king who in his travels met and married a very poor but beautiful woman. Later he was forced to return to his kingdom. When the sons they had had together were grown, the woman sent them to the court of their father. Although they were poorly dressed—as poorly dressed as I and my companions—the king recognized them immediately and brought them into his court with great honour."

The pope smiled down at Francis. "Even so, little brother, will God welcome you and your companions. Go with my blessing, and continue your work."

The brothers were glad to leave the busy streets and grand buildings of Rome for the quiet hills of Assisi. Here the gifts of God were all around them. Francis loved nature so much that he would build nests for the birds and pick up worms from the pathways so they wouldn't be stepped on. The animals responded to his love. Sheep and birds followed him about. He is even said to have tamed a wolf that was killing the people of a nearby town.

Once when he was walking with his friends, they came across a huge flock of birds. Leaving his friends, Francis immediately began to preach to the birds, speaking to them of the many blessings they had. As if they understood, the birds stopped their chirping and gathered around him.

But Francis' sermons were usually directed at people. At first the crowds only jeered at him, but soon people were impressed by his kindness and simple life. They were more willing to listen to him than to proud, wealthy priests because he practised what he preached. He seemed to speak to each one of them, not in fancy words but in simple language that they all understood. He played every part in his stories, even dancing about as he spoke, while his audience laughed, wept and vowed to lead a better life.

Among the people who heard Francis preach was Clare, the daughter of a wealthy noble family. One day she approached the humble friar secretly, asking him to teach her how to serve God.

Francis was delighted. Clare was just the kind of great lady that he had dreamed about when he had wanted to become a knight—young, beautiful, kind and idealistic. And now she too wanted to follow him in a life of dedication to God.

But Clare's family wanted her to marry a wealthy noble. She knew he was probably only interested in how large her dowry was and how many children she could produce to carry on his family name. The life Francis led seemed much more attractive. So one night, after everyone had gone to sleep, she crept out of the huge palace and into the night. At the Portiuncula, the friars welcomed her. There she discarded her jewels and rich clothing, cut off her long blond hair and put on the rough habit of the Friars Minor. Then Francis took her to a nearby convent.

Clare's relatives were furious when they found out what had happened. They tried to persuade her to return, telling her how much they missed her, reminding her of what she was giving up. They even threatened to drag her back to Assisi. But Clare clung to the altar, and even her warlike uncles didn't dare pull her away.

In time, Clare's two sisters, her mother and several of her cousins joined her at San Damiano, where she started her own convent. Eventually the pope gave his approval to Clare and her Poor Ladies, as they were called, as a new order, a female version of Francis' Friars Minor. Through her life she and Francis continued to be close friends, and Francis often turned to her for advice and comfort.

On another occasion Francis' preaching converted a whole town.

Francis wasn't sure how successful he would be with the tough
workers of Cannara. But by the end of his sermon, everyone wanted
to join the Little Brothers or the Poor Ladies.

Francis didn't know what to say to them. He knew that the way he
and his friends lived was a special calling from God. He didn't expect
everyone to live the way he did. And surely it wasn't right to break up
families? Eventually, Francis thought of an answer: a Third Order. Its
members would continue with their families and careers but would
agree to live a simple life, devoting their spare time and money to
helping others. Over the coming centuries many people were able to
develop their talents while trying to live the life of the Gospels through
the Third Order: Michelangelo, Christopher Columbus and Franz
Liszt were among them.

Meanwhile, Francis' followers were preaching and gaining
new members all over Europe. Francis himself decided to go to Egypt,
where the Christian armies were fighting a crusade against the Muslim
troops of Sultan Malik-al-Kamil. People of the time thought of the
crusades, which had been going on for more than 100 years, as a
glorious campaign to regain the holy places of the Middle East. But
Francis saw them for what they were: cruel battles in which God's
children tortured and destroyed each other out of pride and greed.
Wouldn't it be much better if the Sultan and his followers all converted to Christianity?

Francis and one of his companions, Brother Illuminato, set out
across the desert. As they drew near to the sultan's camp, a group of
soldiers seized them. They were about to kill the two men, when they
noticed their strange, coarse clothing. Perhaps they were holy men.
The soldiers debated for a moment, then decided to take the two to the
sultan.

Francis explained to Sultan Malik-al-Kamil that they had come to
convert him to Christianity. "Bring your wisest religious men, and we
will debate with them," he challenged.

The sultan's counsellors wanted no debate. They advised him to cut
off the Christians' heads immediately. But although the sultan could
be as cruel a warrior as his Christian foes, he was also a well-educated
man who enjoyed debating about life and faith. He had quickly

realized that his two visitors were no ordinary men. "Very well," he told them. "Since my own counsellors refuse to debate with you, I will."

And so through the long days and nights that followed, Francis talked with the sultan, explaining Christianity and his own ideas about love. The sultan was impressed, though to Francis' disappointment he did not agree to be converted. When their visit ended, the sultan sent the two men back to the Christian camp with a huge escort, of the sort usually reserved for a king.

But when Francis returned to Italy, he received bad news. During his absence, the brothers had quarrelled. Some of the people Francis had left in charge had started to lead a luxurious life and to build great homes for the brothers. Francis deposed them.

But other brothers had reasonable complaints. They wanted to change the rules of the order. The life was too hard, and some of the rules—such as not being able to carry any money and not being allowed to study—kept them from being as effective as they might be.

The next years were painful for Francis. He yearned for the days when he and a few friends had lived the simple life together at the Portiuncula, when everyone had been equal and everyone had done as he liked.

But what had worked for a small group of friends in one little patch of Italy would not work for thousands of people scattered across Europe. Friends like Bishop Guido and the pope pointed out that it wouldn't serve God's purpose if brothers were forced to leave the order because their faith wasn't as strong as Francis'.

In the end, Francis had to make changes. But he went through agonizing depression. Perhaps God had deserted him. Or perhaps he had just been deluding himself all along. Suddenly, one day, the thought occurred to him: whose order was it, his or God's?

He realized that perhaps it wasn't necessary for him to retain control. He would let someone else become the leader and trust God to guide him. Francis himself would devote the rest of his life to prayer and to counselling the other brothers.

There are many miraculous stories told about Francis. Some sound like legends. Some may be symbolic tales. Others are more believable. But the hardest miracle of all to understand happened in the last years of his life.

Francis was now in his early forties, worn out by illness, his journeys and the many times he had denied himself proper meals. With his closest friends, he decided to go into the mountains to pray and meditate on Jesus' love and sufferings.

Francis found a ridge high up the mountain, where he could be alone. Every day his closest friend, Brother Leo, came to pray with him and make sure he was all right. One day he found Francis looking even more worn out than usual. There were traces of blood on his habit, and he seemed to be trying to hide his hands and feet. Upset by what he saw, Leo immediately demanded to know what had happened.

For a moment Francis hesitated. Then he poured out the story. Just before dawn he had been praying. Suddenly the whole mountain seemed to be covered in light. Looking above him, Francis had seen Jesus on the cross. When he awoke from the vision, he had discovered bloody wounds on his hands and feet and in his side—like the wounds that Christ had suffered. At first he had not wanted to tell anyone about it, but he knew he would need help to bind up these wounds.

A miracle that brings suffering rather than healing is hard to believe. Yet it seems unlikely that a man who had devoted his life to love and perfect honesty would suddenly begin such a difficult deception or that, even if he had, his idealistic friends would have helped him. Many people saw these wounds, which never healed, over the last two years of Francis' life, and the town records of Assisi contain a list of witnesses who swore they saw these marks on his corpse. Francis' case is the first recorded instance of "stigmata" as the marks are called. Other more recent cases have been studied and confirmed by physicians.

Perhaps the best way to understand what happened to Francis is to say that more than anything else in his life he wanted to be like Jesus, and in the end God brought him as close as possible to getting his wish.

By now Francis was nearly blind, too. Thinking back to the troubadours' songs he used to sing in the sun-filled piazzas of Assisi, he decided he would write his own song, praising God instead. Calling together the brothers he sang them his song, thanking God for his brother the sun, for sister moon and the stars, for the wind and water, the fire and the earth. Everywhere they went, he told the brothers, they should sing this song to remind the people of all the good things that came from God.

A short time later, Francis heard that his old friend Bishop Guido was fighting with another friend, the mayor of Assisi. The whole town was in an uproar. The bishop had thrown the mayor out of the Church; the mayor had forbidden anyone to have anything to do with the bishop, even to sell food to his household.

Francis sent a message to his two friends to meet in the piazza where 18 years earlier he had been on trial. As the crowd listened reverently to this message from their dying saint, the brothers sang the *Canticle of Brother Sun*.

But Francis had added a new verse:

Be praised, my lord, for those who grant pardon for love of you,
And bear sickness and tribulation.
Blessed are they who shall bear them in peace,
For by You, Most High, they shall be crowned.

As the song ended, the bishop and the mayor embraced before the whole crowd.

Francis sang his song even as he was dying. Some of the brothers were scandalized, but Francis only replied that he couldn't help but be happy when he was so close to being with God.

As everyone expected, Francis was declared a saint in 1228, two years after his death.

Today Francis is honoured as the patron saint of peace, animals, ecology and Italy. Though questions about the proper life for a Franciscan continued, the order grew. Franciscans were the first missionaries to reach China, and they were with Christopher Columbus on his second voyage to the New World. Today not only Roman Catholics are Franciscans; Lutherans, Episcopalians and Anglicans also follow the example of *Il Poverello*.

WILLIAM WILBERFORCE

A voice for freedom

WILLIAM WILBERFORCE

The lost ship *Zong* lay quietly on the windless Caribbean sea. Its strange, fetid stench could be smelled more than a mile away. Watching from the decks, the sailors sometimes saw the fins of the sharks that had followed them all the way from Africa. Occasionally the groans of the slaves below rose to the decks.

At first the Africans had been terrified—stolen from their villages or captured in war, then herded to the coast to be sold to white men. But now, after 100 days of lying in chains in a dark hold with their own waste washing about them, each jammed into a space smaller than a coffin, they were too miserable to feel fear.

The *Zong*'s captain was worried. Usually about 10 percent of a cargo of slaves would die on a trip, but already he had lost 60 slaves and seven crewmen. The ship's water was running low. By the time he found Jamaica, the slaves who survived would be too weak to fetch a good price. He knew that the owners of the vast sugar plantations in the British colonies wanted strong slaves who could work 11 hours a day under the steady bite of the whip.

But the captain had a solution. If the slaves simply died or failed to get good prices, the merchants who had organized the slaving trip would lose money. But if the captain claimed that the slaves were becoming violent and had to be killed to save the ship, then the insurance company would have to pay for the loss.

The slaves were brought on deck, blinking in the sunlight and gasping in fresh air. At first they thought they had been brought out for exercise. Then the sailors herded them to the side of the boat. Amid the screaming, the sailors began to push the slaves overboard.

One hundred and thirty-two black men and women were thrown into the sea.

When the insurance company protested, the judge who heard the case replied that since the slaves were the property of the slavers, they could do what they wanted with their human cargo; it was "exactly as if horses had been thrown overboard."

The *Zong* was typical of English ships that carried as many as 50,000 slaves a year from Africa to the British colonies. English ships had carried Africans to the West Indies and brought back sugar since about 1663. And for almost as long, men and women who realized it was wrong spoke against it. But it wasn't until the case of the *Zong*, in 1783, that a group banded together to try to stop the slave trade.

Owning slaves was illegal in Britain itself. But to stop British ships from dealing in slaves for the colonies, a law would have to be passed by Parliament. The group needed a leader—someone young and energetic, a persuasive speaker and expert politician.

On a bright December morning in 1785, a silent, well-dressed young man walked round and round a small square in London. When anyone walked by, he turned his head or stared down at the sidewalk. If any of the people passing had recognized him, they would have been surprised to see one of the country's most popular young men and skilful politicians skulking about Charles Square like a pickpocket.

At 26, William Wilberforce seemed to have everything. He was heir to a large fortune. He was also the member of Parliament for Yorkshire, one of the most important seats in the House of Commons. He and the prime minister, William Pitt, were like brothers; some people even thought that Wilberforce himself would be prime minister someday.

But William Wilberforce had recently had an experience that changed his future. On a trip to France with an old friend who was a Christian, he suddenly saw the uselessness of his life. He wanted to serve God, but he didn't know how. Should he give up the brilliant career that lay before him?

In his confusion, he decided to visit a friend from his childhood. The Reverend John Newton was a minister with an interesting past. Before his conversion, he had been the captain of a slaving ship and even for a while a slave himself. But now "the Old African Blasphemer," as he liked to call himself, was a popular preacher, who even wrote his own hymns, such as "Amazing Grace."

But he was also an Evangelical, one of the Britons who criticized the loose standards of society and of the established church and who wanted to bring people closer to God.

Newton and his kind were despised by the sophisticated upper classes. Wilberforce himself had often made fun of the Evangelicals. If word got out that he had become one of them, his career might be ruined.

Finally, he made up his mind and walked to the door of the manse.

After Wilberforce explained his problem, the grizzled old man sat in silence, considering the young man before him. He had money, important friends and political skill. But he had something more, a kind of sunshine that made people want to be with him and follow him. Newton said: "You must keep your seat in Parliament. The Lord has raised you up for the good of his church and for the good of his nation."

But what was that good to be? Newton himself offered a clue, with his stories of the miseries of the slave trade. Wilberforce talked with the men and women who were involved in the fight against slavery. They urged him to join them. So did his friend William Pitt, the prime minister, even though he knew it would cause political problems for both of them.

Although they opposed slavery as a whole, Wilberforce and his friends decided to start by working to abolish the slave trade. But first they had to gather evidence. There were no statistics easily available, and aside from John Newton and James Ramsay, a clergyman who had lived in the West Indies, they had no eyewitness accounts. Several people, including Thomas Clarkson, a young man who had given up his plans to become a minister in order to join the fight, set to work gathering an astounding amount of information. Clarkson travelled all over England, searching out sailors. Once he interviewed 3,000 seamen in order to find one witness. He was often threatened by the captains and crew of slaving ships. And James Ramsay was slandered so much by the press and the traders because he spoke out against the slave trade that his health broke down and he died.

Meanwhile, Wilberforce prepared to start the campaign in Parliament.

Many members of the House of Commons owned property in the West Indies or made money from slaving voyages. They tried to prove that the trade was necessary and that slaves did not suffer. But the rest of the House was shocked by the stories told by the abolitionists: the nine-month-old baby who was beaten to death by the captain of a slaving ship; the epidemics that killed both slaves and seamen; the blacks who were left to die on the docks because they were too weak to be sold.

The greatest orators of the day spoke against the trade, including the prime minister and the leader of the Opposition. Wilberforce himself made a speech that some people said was the best that had ever been heard in the House of Commons. But in the end, as one observer put it, the pygmies won against the giants. The debate first started in 1789, but the supporters of the trade managed to delay a vote until 1791. After two years of constant work by the abolitionists, the bill to end the slave trade was defeated, 163 to 88.

Many politicians might have given up at this point. Wilberforce did not. But he knew now that the battle would be longer and harder than he had realized.

I t is hard to understand today how British politicians and the public could allow the slave trade and slavery to continue for so long. Part of the reason was financial. Britain depended greatly on her colonies and trade for her wealth. People were afraid that without slavery the British economy would be ruined. They thought about slavery much the way we think about eating meat. We don't like the idea of animals being slaughtered, yet we believe that meat is necessary in our diet. So we try not to think about the animals we kill. In the same way, people of the 18th century saw slavery and the slave trade as necessary evils.

People in Wilberforce's time were also concerned about property. They believed that protecting property was the basis of liberty. If the government could take away what belonged to a person, then nothing would be safe. Slaves were property; a slave trader or plantation owner had paid for them. People didn't want to take away that property, even if they felt slavery was unjust.

There was no television to show the British people the appalling conditions of the slave trade. As well, many people in England lived under conditions almost as bad as those of slaves. Children worked in the mines and factories for 10 hours a day. People were hanged for the smallest crimes, while others were transported to work in Australia.

The abolitionists worked hard to change public opinion. They wrote pamphlets and organized anti-slavery societies, and they presented huge petitions to the government.

One event nearly killed their campaign. In 1793 the French cut off

the heads of their king, Louis XVI, and his wife, Marie Antoinette.
The bloody French Revolution was under way. Many people feared
that the revolution would spread to Britain; others realized their country would soon be at war with France. As a result, English politicians
were more afraid than ever of doing anything to antagonize the
colonies, harm Britain's economy or encourage revolt among the
slaves.

But even though the campaign against the slave trade was
becalmed, Wilberforce kept busy. Though he was conservative about
political and social change in England, he founded and led hundreds
of charitable organizations. And he was writing a book.

When *A Practical View of Christianity* was published in 1797, it
sold out in a few days and remained a bestseller for 50 years.

Wilberforce had written the book to explain to his friends what he
believed and to convince people that they should lead a more Christian
life. It was not enough to go to church on Sunday and be a nice person
the rest of the week, he argued. A true Christian should allow
religion into every part of life. His book, combined with the example of his own life, persuaded thousands of people to take their
Christianity more seriously.

Wilberforce and his closest friends practised what they preached.
His cousin, Henry Thornton, bought a large home in a village named
Clapham, just outside London, and invited Wilberforce to live there.
Soon, others who also wanted to be full-time Christians and fight the
evils of society came to Clapham. Some came for long visits. Others
bought houses, married into each other's families and raised their
children together.

On a typical Sunday, they would gather in the library of Thornton's
home. Granville Sharp, the man who had forced the courts to decide
that slavery was illegal in Britain, might bring up the subject of Sierra
Leone, the colony in Africa that they had founded for the freed slaves.
Charles Grant, a businessman who had lived in India, would suggest
ways of getting the government to let them send missionaries to that
country. Those who had seats in Parliament would discuss legislation
to reform the prisons and restrict child labour.

At the centre of everything was Wilberforce, enchanting everyone with his stories and humour. If the conversation became too serious, he would be off into the bright garden to play with the children or chase after a cat. One friend said once that "he frisked about as if every vein in his body was filled with quicksilver."

But the conversation always came back to the subject that was most important to Wilberforce and his supporters. While the others continued their research and tried to rouse public opinion, Wilberforce proposed motions for the abolition of the slave trade in the House of Commons year after discouraging year. Once, Wilberforce lost only because some of the people who had promised to support him had gone to see a new opera instead.

Even in 1805, after the war with France ended and more members of Parliament seemed in favour of abolition, Wilberforce and his supporters in Parliament, nicknamed the "Saints," were disappointed. Many of the members who had promised to support the bill were absent. Once again, Wilberforce's bill to abolish the slave trade was defeated, this time by 77 votes to 70.

As he left the House of Commons on the night of his defeat, one of the officials spoke to him. "Mr. Wilberforce, you shouldn't expect to carry a measure of this kind," he said. "You and I have seen enough of life to know that people will not vote for something that will hurt them in the pocket."

"I do expect to carry it," Wilberforce replied, "and what is more, I feel assured I will carry it speedily."

But that night he had nightmares about the slaves being whipped into ships on the coast of Africa. While Parliament delayed, thousands of people were being tortured and killed. He felt more discouraged than he ever had before. Would victory ever come?

Bright candles flickered above the green carpets in the House of Commons on the night of February 23, 1807. Something amazing was happening. After 20 years of indifference to the slave trade, suddenly there was a change. Speaker after speaker was supporting abolition.

As soon as one sat down, eight others would be on their feet, demanding to be heard.

Wilberforce sat in a trance. With a new generation of members committed to abolition, he had known they had a better chance. But he hadn't expected this. "How God can change the hearts of men," he thought to himself.

Now all attention was focused on the Solicitor General, Sir Samuel Romilly, who was coming to the climax of his speech. Many people believed that Napoleon, the conqueror of Europe, was the greatest man of the age, said Romilly. Yet he must be tortured by guilt over the bloodshed and suffering he had caused. How different must be the feelings of his "honourable friend"—everyone knew whom he meant—"How much more pure happiness must he enjoy, knowing that he has saved the lives of so many people...."

At this point, the whole House rose to its feet, cheering and applauding. Wilberforce sat with his head in his hands, tears streaming down his face. Never before had the House of Commons cheered any man this way.

When the vote was taken, the House of Commons passed the bill to abolish the slave trade by 283 to 16.

The next stage was obvious: to abolish slavery itself. But that was not easy. At first Wilberforce and his friends thought that slavery would wither away. Plantation owners would be forced to treat their slaves better, since they couldn't get any more. Eventually they would see that free labourers were better than slaves.

But that didn't happen. The plantation owners mistreated their slaves just as much as ever. The men who had fought for the abolition of the slave trade were getting old and discouraged.

Wilberforce, worn by poor health and financial troubles, handed over his leadership in Parliament to Thomas Fowell Buxton, a brother-in-law of Elizabeth Fry. Buxton and other younger men, many of them the sons of the original campaigners, brought new energy to the fight. But sometimes Wilberforce's friends worried that the old man would never live to see the end of slavery.

It had taken 20 years to abolish the slave trade. By 1833, the fight against slavery itself had been going on for another 26 years.

On a summer day that year, the old man had a visit from Thomas Macaulay, the son of one of his closest friends in the long campaign against slavery. Wilberforce's wife, Barbara, wheeled him into the garden, wrapped in huge blankets that made him look smaller than ever. But his eyes were still bright and cheerful.

"You've heard the news?" Macaulay asked. Parliament had agreed to pass a bill that would set all slaves in the British colonies free in a year's time. In return, the planters would get a money settlement.

"Yes. Thank God that I should have lived to witness a day in which England is willing to give 20 million sterling for the abolition of slavery." (Today that would be more than $1 billion.)

The two men chatted about the long campaign. Then Wilberforce left the garden he loved for the last time. Shortly after, in the early morning of July 29, 1833, William Wilberforce died at the age of 73.

Far away in Africa, jungle drums carried the news. Britain gave him a state funeral, with a statue in Westminster Abbey. In London, every third person seemed to wear some token of mourning, and blacks everywhere, both slave and free, honoured his death.

But the tribute he would have cared for most came a year later. At midnight on July 31, 1834, 800,000 men and women were set free.

ELIZABETH FRY

Doing miracles of mercy

ELIZABETH FRY

The jailors tried to talk Mrs. Fry out of entering the women's ward. Even Governor Newman was afraid to go in without guards.

But they soon saw it was no use. Despite her plain, dark clothes and prim white Quaker cap, this tall woman moved as if she were the Queen herself, and in her hand she held a letter of permission from the Governor of Newgate Prison in London to visit the women's section of the prison.

As the turnkeys opened the heavy iron gates, the stink of dampness, unwashed bodies and urine slapped against her face. The yard was filled with an unearthly din. Some prisoners banged on the outer bars, whining at passersby for money to buy liquor. Dirty children scrabbled in the dust, and two half-naked women, ignored by the others, rolled on the ground, scratching, spitting and tearing at each other's hair.

Suddenly the noise stopped. The prisoners had spotted her. As the women crowded around, all the guards could see of her was the top of her white bonnet. They reached for the keys, ready to rush in and rescue her before the prisoners could tear her to shreds.

But their help wasn't needed. As the astonished guards watched, the prisoners began to weep.

It was a strange situation for a daughter of the Gurney family. For the first 18 years of her life, Elizabeth would never have worn the plain, dull clothes of a Quaker, let alone enter a dirty and dangerous prison.

The Gurneys were Quakers, a sect that had once been persecuted for its beliefs in equality, a simple life and pacifism. But because Quakers didn't waste their time or their money, they often did well in business. By the late 18th century, the Gurneys were one of the wealthiest families in England. John Gurney's handsome and spirited children were favourites in the highest society. Though they still attended the local Quaker meetings, they saw no reason to wear drab clothes or shun dancing and parties the way the strict Quakers did.

To outsiders, Betsy, with her tall figure and blond good looks, seemed much the same as her six sisters and four brothers. But Betsy felt she was different. She wasn't strong and courageous, clever and self-confident, like the others. She was often sick and afraid—of nightmares, water, death. She longed to do something worthwhile with her life, but didn't know what.

All the Gurney children hated the stuffy Quaker meetings. There was no minister. Men and women sat silently, until someone was inspired to say something—usually something boring! Betsy certainly never felt inspired by these services of worship. Sometimes she was not even sure that God existed at all.

But at other times, when she was writing in her diary, she wondered if she could be a better person by believing in God. "I think anybody who had a real faith could never be unhappy," she wrote. She thought of faith as "the only certain source of support and comfort in this life, and what is best of all, it draws to virtue...."

One Sunday morning the Gurney girls settled into their places with the usual rustling of silks. The disapproving stares levelled by strict and stodgy old Quakers around them only made them feel more pleased with themselves. Especially Betsy, who had put on her new boots, purple laced with scarlet. No wonder the old Quakers frowned!

Betsy spent the first part of the meeting admiring her feet, turning them this way and that.

Then an American visitor, William Savery, began to speak, and

Betsy forgot all about her new boots. Quakers today were not as dedicated as they had been 100 years ago, he said. Then they had been willing to go to prison for what they believed. Nowadays, he wondered if they believed in anything. The "heathen" Indians whom Savery had worked with showed more interest in God than some of the "Christians" he had met in England.

Betsy joked and laughed with her sisters after the meeting, but inside she was thinking hard.

Over the next few weeks, Betsy had many chances to talk with William Savery. She began to see that there was more to being a Quaker than she had realized. Friends like William Savery certainly didn't lead boring lives; many spent their time helping others and promoting peace. There was even a point to their simple lifestyle, Betsy recognized. If she dressed more simply and avoided parties she would have more time to do something worthwhile, and she wouldn't feel so envious so often or do the silly things she was always sorry for later.

Soon her family saw a change in Betsy. She began to wear the plain clothes of the Quakers and visit the poor and sick in the neighbourhood. She started a school for 70 children in the Gurney's laundry room.

At first, her sisters made fun of her. They thought she was pretending to be a better person than they were. Betsy, who was more open-minded about her religion than most people of her time, tried to explain that her new way of living made it easier for her to be the kind of person she wanted to be. It didn't necessarily mean that everyone else had to live that way.

Slowly her family grew to understand her. They could see that she was happier and easier to get along with.

They didn't have long to appreciate the new Betsy. In 1800, when she was 20, she married Joseph Fry, the son of a wealthy but strict Quaker family, and moved from the country to London. There she was expected to hold open house for the Fry family and all their Quaker friends and visitors, as well as looking after her own children. She and Joseph had 11 children altogether.

Though Betsy Fry's life was full and happy, there were times when she felt dissatisfied. She loved her family, but what had become of her ambitions to do something worthwhile? "I fear that my life is slipping away to little purpose," she confided to her diary.

Then, one day in 1813, a Quaker friend came to see her about a problem he had discovered. He had been to Newgate Prison and visited the women's quarters. Although it was a particularly cold January, many of the women and their children, some of whom were sick, didn't have enough clothes. They didn't even have enough straw to lie on at night.

With her quick common sense, Betsy immediately sent messages to friends, then went out to buy material. That afternoon, the women made up baby clothing. The next morning, Betsy and her friend Anna Buxton went to Newgate. The reluctant guard led them through gloomy halls to the women's quarters. There they found nearly 300 women—from experienced criminals to untried girls—crowded into two rooms. The women, many of them drunk, gambled for money to buy alcohol or fought among themselves. Two were stripping the clothing from a dead baby.

Even hardened male prisoners were disgusted by the behaviour of the women. But if Betsy and Anna were shocked, they did not show it. They set to work at once, and within a few hours, every baby had been properly clothed.

But there was still much work to be done. The next two days the ladies were back again, with clothes for the adults and clean straw for the sick. On the last visit, Betsy and Anna knelt to pray with the women.

Betsy longed to do more, but her growing family kept her too busy. It was four years before she was able to go back to Newgate.

When the gates clanged shut behind her, Betsy Fry found herself surrounded by the women prisoners. She knew she was in danger. She must find some way of appealing to them, something they had in common.

Her eyes fell on a little boy, pale and dressed in rags, and she

thought of her own baby boy at home. Picking the child up, she turned to the women. "Friends," she said, "many of you are mothers. I
too am a mother. I am distressed for your children."

She paused and looked into their eyes. They were listening.

"Is there not something we can do for these innocent little ones? Do
you want them to grow up to become prisoners themselves? Are they
to learn to be thieves and worse?"

She had chosen exactly the right words. Despite their degradation,
the women still cared for their children. And she spoke as if they were
human beings like herself, and asked them what they thought! No one
in Newgate had ever done that before.

The stunned women began to weep. Someone brought Mrs. Fry a
chair, and soon the stories began to spill out—fears for their children,
anger at people who had betrayed them, the desperate poverty that
had driven them to crime. Betsy prayed with them and read from the
Bible, telling them about a mysterious person named Jesus. Some had
heard of him, but others had not.

When she left, Betsy promised to be back the next day—so they
could make plans.

The first thing to be done, the women agreed, was to educate their
children. They chose one well-educated woman to be the teacher.
Betsy felt encouraged, but she warned the prisoners that she could do
nothing without the approval of the prison authorities.

The authorities thought Mrs. Fry meant well. But she did not know
Newgate as they did, they explained. Her school would come to
nothing. Besides, there was no room for it.

Betsy persisted. If she could find a room, would they allow her to
start the school? Grudgingly, the authorities agreed.

Soon she was back. The prisoners had agreed to give up one of their
rooms. Now could she start? They could not refuse.

The only problem with the school was its instant success.
Children and younger prisoners were soon learning to read and write.
But many women also wanted to learn. A third of them could only
read a little and another third not at all. They also wanted to learn to
sew, so that they could make clothes for themselves and their children.

Betsy realized that one reason prisoners became so depressed and dissolute in prison was that they were bored. If they could learn to read and write and could acquire some skills, they would feel busy and develop more self-respect. They could earn money and perhaps even support themselves after they were released.

Betsy planned a school for the women as well. They would be organized into small groups, each supervised by a monitor. As well as learning to read and write, they would make items for sale.

But when she went to two of her brothers-in-law for help, they rejected the idea. Both Samuel Hoare and Thomas Fowell Buxton were involved in prison reform, so they knew what prisoners could be like. The women would steal the materials and sell them to buy drink, they said. They advised her to go back to her family and leave prison reform to men.

Betsy decided that when it came to prison reform, women understood other women a lot better than men did. So she gathered a group of female friends to support her plans. Several Quaker merchants donated sewing materials. A company that supplied quilts and clothing to Australia agreed to sell everything the prisoners could turn out.

Now all she had to do was convince the prison authorities.

She called a meeting of the women prisoners and invited the governor and other directors. At the meeting, Betsy explained to more than 70 prisoners that everything depended on them. They would be consulted about the running of the school, but if they didn't stick to the rules, the whole project would fail.

The women, carefully coached beforehand, approved all the rules unanimously.

Within a few weeks the prisoners had proved the pessimists wrong. People who came to seem them were amazed. Instead of dirty, swearing wenches, they found groups of neatly dressed, well-mannered women busily working, while one of their number read aloud. "Already from being like wild beasts," Betsy wrote, "the prisoners appear harmless and kind."

The prison authorities began to admit that these prisoners might really be human after all. They adopted Betsy's reforms as part of the Newgate system, covering part of the costs for the school and for better food and clothing.

Now every day in Newgate started with a Bible reading. Most of the prisoners believed in God, though they knew little about religion. Bible stories, totally new to many of them, were fascinating and gave them hope that God loved them and forgave them and would help them to change their lives.

It was especially easy to believe this when Mrs. Fry read. Betsy had a beautiful voice and had become an experienced speaker at Quaker meetings, where men and women were treated as equals. To her family she was "just a wife and mother," but in front of an audience she had an unusual ability to sway emotions, like a great actress.

The upper classes were equally fascinated. News of Mrs. Fry's success was spreading through London. Many people were eager to see the "miracles" at Newgate. It became fashionable to attend Mrs. Fry's readings. The American ambassador wrote home that he had seen the two greatest sights in London: St. Paul's Cathedral and Mrs. Fry's Bible reading.

At first, Betsy was disturbed by seeing dukes, bishops and high-born ladies present. It was supposed to be a private worship service for prisoners. All those grand people seemed to her to be "making a show of a good thing." But she decided it was worthwhile for the publicity. People with influence would see how well-behaved and sincere the prisoners could be and what hard conditions they lived in.

The strategy worked. By 1818, only two years after her return to Newgate, Betsy Fry's work had become so famous that she was asked

to appear before a House of Commons committee investigating London prisons. She was the first woman—other than a queen—to speak to a committee on a major issue.

In speaking to the committee, she emphasized four points. First, prisoners should have work to do and, second, a chance to study the Bible. Third, prisons for women should have female warders. (It was hard on a woman's self-respect to have men watching her when she needed privacy. And in some cases, women became prostitutes, to get special favours from the guards.) Fourth, women should be divided into different classes, depending on the crimes they had committed and how long they had been criminals, so that the young and sometimes innocent would not be corrupted by more experienced criminals. And finally, she recommended improvements in prison conditions.

The committee was impressed. Many of the reforms Betsy suggested were included in the Prison Act of 1823.

Letters came from all over Britain asking for advice. Betsy began to tour through the country, visiting prisons and making reports to local authorities. Most of the prisons were dark, dirty, airless and overcrowded. In one jail built to hold 110 prisoners, she found nearly 1,700 people.

There were no laws to enforce her recommendations, so she had to rely on tact and persuasion.

Because she couldn't be everywhere at once to see that reforms were carried out, in the evenings she held meetings for ladies who were interested in prison visiting. The response was amazing. In Aberdeen she expected only a few women; more than 200 showed up.

Everywhere she went, Betsy emphasized her four principles. But the most important thing, she told the women's committees, was to treat the prisoners like human beings. "Much depends on the spirit in which the worker enters upon her work," she explained. "It must be in the spirit not of judgment but of mercy. She must not say in her heart, 'I am holier than thou.'"

She advised workers not to discuss the criminals' past, for "we have all come short." Rather, they should emphasize the future, helping the women to make plans to improve their situation and rewarding good behaviour.

And above all, the ladies "must not be impatient if they find the work of reformation a very slow one."

Within a few years every major prison in Great Britain had a visiting society, and in 1821 a central organization was established, the Ladies' British Society for Promoting the Reformation of Female Prisoners.

Meanwhile, Betsy continued to visit Newgate Prison whenever she was in London. One day she noticed that the guards looked worried. They explained that tomorrow a group of women would be put on board ship, to be transported to Australia. At that time Britain was using its southern colony as a dumping place for criminals.

The guards hated these nights before the women left. The despairing prisoners would get drunk, break everything they could and often set fires.

Betsy understood why. Even getting to the ship was a terrible experience. First the women were shackled and moved in open carts, with a jeering, mud-slinging crowd all around them. Then they would be crowded into dirty, dark quarters down in the belly of the ship. During the eight-month journey to Australia they were hardly ever allowed into the fresh air or given anything to do. Often there weren't enough food or washing supplies to keep themselves healthy.

Betsy immediately went to Governor Newman, now one of her greatest admirers, and got his promise that the women would be moved unchained in closed coaches. Then she spent the evening with the women, comforting them.

The next morning, when Betsy came to go with the women to the docks, they calmly said good-bye to their fellow-prisoners, who had taken up a collection for them out of their small savings.

Once on board, the women still had to wait for more than a month until other women prisoners arrived from all over England. Meanwhile, Betsy and her friends did what they could to make the coming journey less horrible. They organized the women and children into classes and work groups, just as in Newgate, and gave them sewing supplies as well as extra clothing. Until they set sail, Betsy visited them. On the last day, curious sailors climbed the rigging to watch in perfect silence as Mrs. Fry read from her Bible and then knelt on the deck of the ship to ask a blessing.

Over the next 23 years, Betsy visited and organized almost every women's transport ship that left London—106 ships and 12,000 convicts altogether. She and her supporters were responsible for legislation that women could no longer be put in irons, that children under seven could travel with their mothers and that no woman could be transported if she was nursing a child. It was a brave captain who could withstand a stern gaze from Mrs. Fry or her Quaker friends if supplies were inadequate or the ship was not well-kept. The women themselves received small but important comforts—more soap, books and frequent trips on deck for fresh air and exercise. Betsy also used her influence to see that the women were better cared for when they arrived in Australia.

But miserable as the voyage to Australia was, transported prisoners were lucky compared to those condemned to die. Betsy and her helpers often visited these women during their last hours, trying to give them courage. One woman was pregnant with her eighth child. As soon as the child was born, she was executed. Another woman was convicted of helping in a robbery. The night before she was to be hanged, the robber admitted that she was innocent. She was hanged anyway.

Betsy tried to get pardons for women, but she was not always successful. To bring public attention to the situation, she encouraged the newspapers to publish stories about the condemned prisoners.

At that time, more than 200 crimes were punishable by death. Many were petty crimes—stealing a pair of stockings or a coat, or poaching. As Betsy's brother-in-law Thomas Buxton said in a speech in Parliament, it didn't matter whether you killed your father or somebody's rabbit; the penalty was the same. Urged on by Betsy, relatives and friends like Buxton and William Wilberforce argued in Parliament that only murder deserved the death penalty. Betsy herself believed that executions should be abolished altogether.

As a result of the public outcry, by the mid 1800s only 16 crimes were still punishable by death.

But reform came slowly. The Industrial Revolution brought drastic changes to the lives of working people, as they moved to the factories and cities. Families split up, people lost their jobs, and even those who had jobs often lived in appalling slums. For many, drinking was the only escape. Despite severe punishments, the crime rate leaped.

In these conditions, Betsy Fry continued to oppose harsh punishment for criminals. "I believe kindness does more in turning them from the error of their ways than harsh treatment," she told a Commons committee.

But though Betsy had figures to back up her methods—the number of women who came back to Newgate had dropped by more than 40 percent—she was speaking against the spirit of her times. Stern, self-righteous reformers believed people committed crimes simply because they were wicked. The only way to stop crime was to scare criminals, by making punishment harsher.

A minister at St. Paul's Cathedral summed up the typical view: "There must be a great deal of solitude, coarse food, a dress of shame, hard, incessant, irksome external labour, a planned and regulated and unrelenting exclusion of happiness and comfort." These people did not believe that other humans could be driven to crime because they were hungry, desperate or corrupted by the horrible conditions they lived in. Mrs. Fry and her methods were considered soft.

Betsy also had critics closer to home. In those days people believed that a woman's place was in her home—and nowhere else. Her fellow Quakers and some relatives criticized Betsy for not paying more attention to her family.

Fortunately her husband Joseph was an unusually understanding man. But in 1828 his business, along with many others, went bankrupt. Betsy's wealthy Gurney relatives came to their rescue, but the Quakers, who placed a high value on their business integrity, thought Joseph Fry's failure reflected badly on them and so they kicked him out of their local congregation. Betsy was deeply hurt. Her children, already as restless at meetings as their mother had once been, began to drift away from the Quaker sect. This wounded Betsy even more. Yet she could hardly blame the children. And she realized that you didn't have to be a Quaker to be a Christian.

Though Betsy's efforts at reforming prisons fell on hard times at home, abroad she was famous. Letters came from kings and queens across Europe, asking how they could reform their prisons. As far away as St. Petersburg in Russia, ladies of the aristocracy formed visiting committees and pressed for more humane treatment.

Eventually, Betsy decided to visit the prisoners of Europe for herself. Between 1838 and 1843 she went to the continent five times, visiting France, Switzerland, Belgium, Germany, the Netherlands and Denmark.

Everywhere she went, even when she could not speak the local language, her musical voice had its usual magical effect. In Berlin, the Crown Princess organized the first meeting of the ladies' committee at the palace. The King of Prussia immediately made reforms in his country's prisons.

Sticking to Quaker beliefs, Betsy treated all her royal friends as her equals. Yet she was always on the watch for the vanity she had felt when she was a teenager. Every time she was cheered at a meeting or praised by some crowned head of Europe, she tried to remind herself that her success was God's work, not hers.

It was especially hard not to feel pleased with herself on a day in 1842, when the King of Prussia came to call at her home in London. Many were scandalized that a monarch would visit a commoner's house. Others were upset that a Quaker would entertain on so grand a scale.

First she and the King visited Newgate Prison, where in her prayers Betsy reminded everyone of another, more important king. Then she welcomed the Prussian to the Fry home.

Betsy may have laughed to herself about the girl in the scarlet and purple boots 44 years before. She had given up all that to live the simple, humble life of a Quaker. Yet serving God had brought her a more exciting life than if she had never changed. Now her friends ranged from Queen Victoria to the lowliest thief in the bottom of a ship bound for Australia.

She couldn't have imagined how many more friends would come in the future, when governments around the world saw the wisdom of a

prison system that wasn't based on revenge, and when thousands of
other women would carry on the work of visiting prisons and helping
ex-convicts, often naming their organizations after Elizabeth Fry.

FATHER DAMIEN

Serving the living dead

FATHER DAMIEN

Damien danced around his older brother's sickbed.

"I'm going, Pamphile," he cried joyfully, "I'm going in your place!"

Pamphile groaned. He was the one who was supposed to go to Hawaii. It was 1863, and his order, the Fathers of the Sacred Heart, desperately needed missionaries. But he had fallen sick—and now his 23-year-old younger brother had got himself appointed to Hawaii instead. Between pain and disappointment, he wasn't too pleased.

Nor was Father Wenceslas, the head of the community in France where the two brothers from Belgium were studying to be priests. Damien, headstrong as usual, hadn't asked Father Wenceslas' advice. He had written directly to the head of the order: since his brother Pamphile was sick with typhus and couldn't go, could he, Damien, go instead? The Father General had agreed, even though Damien had not yet completed his studies.

Father Wenceslas had thrown the letter of approval in front of Damien at dinner. "You're very young and green to become a missionary when you're not even a priest yet!" he said.

Pamphile wondered how his younger brother would succeed as a missionary. He was popular and always eager to take on harder tasks, and his training on the family farm in Belgium would be useful. But some people thought he laughed too much and too loudly for the dignity of a Sacred Hearts Father. Pamphile didn't mind his brother's bluntness, but others found him tactless. Sometimes in his eagerness Damien lost his temper with other students because he thought they weren't strong enough in their beliefs. But he was always sorry afterward. Perhaps the rough life of a missionary would be the best thing for him.

Bishop Maigret, the head of the Sacred Hearts Fathers in Hawaii, wasn't concerned that Damien hadn't finished his studies. In those green Pacific islands with their rough terrain, restless volcanos and violent storms, no one cared how well a priest spoke Latin or understood the finer points of theology. Shortly after he arrived in Honolulu, Damien was ordained as a priest and sent to work on the island of Hawaii, the huge volcanic island that gave its name to the whole chain.

Damien's district was huge, covering 1,000 square miles (2,600 square kilometres). It took him six weeks to make a complete tour on horseback, visiting the 2,000 people who lived in scattered villages. When one Hawaiian asked the priest where he lived, Damien pointed to his saddle and said, "There's my home." To get to one of the villages, Damien had to cross 10 ravines and then climb a 2,000-foot (600-metre) cliff.

The Hawaiians liked the stocky, rugged priest. He was learning their language quickly; if he couldn't think of the right word he would stop to blow his nose, while the Hawaiians tactfully hid their smiles.

Damien realized how important it was to the Catholics in each village to have their own chapel. His superiors back in Honolulu were bombarded with requests for lumber and building supplies. The Hawaiians built the churches themselves—about one a year during the time Damien was on Hawaii—with the priest acting as architect, foreman and chief worker.

Because he had spent many years helping his father on the family farm, Damien knew about agriculture and business as well as building. He raised animals and grew crops and sold them to buy supplies. The Mother Superior of the Sacred Hearts Sisters often received unexpected shipments of food from him. He knew she hadn't asked for them, Damien would write, but everyone needed potatoes, and the price would be going up in a few weeks. Besides, he wanted to build a new chapel. The Mother Superior always smiled and paid.

Damien's superiors were sometimes exasperated by the way he took things into his own hands, but they were pleased with the results. He baptized many people, sometimes more than 50 a year. The Hawaiians were gentle and friendly, and Damien thought of them as his children: "I love my Hawaiians very much," he wrote in one letter. "They in turn love me as children love their father and mother. I hope this mutual affection will bring about their conversion. If they love their priest, they will easily love our Lord, since the priest is His minister."

Catholic missionaries were not the first white people to come to the Hawaiian islands. Early explorers and traders had landed there, bringing disease and vice. Protestant missionaries from New England had come in the early 19th century to try to protect the natives and to teach them to cope with the new ways of white people. But their children had become powerful merchants or bought vast plantations, and many had become deeply involved in island politics.

Hawaiians resented the increasing control of white people. They especially disliked the times when whites broke up their families and shipped relatives away to a kind of prison camp on the island of Molokai.

As Damien travelled through his district, he would sometimes see human figures stirring in the bushes. A brief glimpse of ravaged, distorted faces—then they would vanish. They were hiding in the mountains from white men who would take them away because they had leprosy.

Although leprosy (Hansen's disease) can now be controlled, at that time there was no cure. Usually the first clear sign was the loss of feeling in parts of the body. The disease quickly spread, causing more numbness and huge open sores. Eyebrows dropped off, and lumps appeared on the victim's face, as if huge worms were burrowing under his skin. Some cases mysteriously cleared up. Other victims might survive a long time. But most died within a few years, tortured by the shame of their appearance as much as by the disease.

Though the disease was hideous, Hawaiians cared for their

stricken friends and relatives at home. But leprosy was contagious (though not as contagious as people at that time believed). Between 10 and 15 percent of the population were stricken.

Some officials feared the entire native population would be wiped out. The government decided that leprosy victims had to be kept separate from the rest of the population in some isolated spot.

They chose the island of Molokai, where a spit of land jutted into the ocean, cut off from the rest of the island by mountains. The Board of Health that created this prison meant well; its members wanted to safeguard the Hawaiian people. But on Molokai they created a living hell.

No decent administrator would stay there for long; those who did mistreated the patients. Doctors visited only occasionally and never stayed long.

Unlike the rest of the islands, the colony was often cold and wet. The patients—if they had a shelter at all—lived in rickety grass shacks. Each person had only one set of clothes to last the year. Supplies of food and medicine came only when the weather was good.

The people in the colony, separated from their families and afflicted with a fatal disease, gave in to despair. "In this place there is no law," sufferers were told when they landed. Strong patients stole food and clothing from the weak. At night there were orgies and wild drinking.

Sometimes as he rode through his district, Damien would think of these people, who had no priest to tell them of God's love and help them to die in dignity. He had seen the listless, despairing victims rounded up to be shipped to the island that they called "the corpse pit." He had spoken to priests who had visited Molokai and left weeping uncontrollably at the suffering they had seen. The victims of leprosy were under sentence of death.

But aren't we all? Damien thought. Life on earth was only a brief stay, before we left to be with God. Couldn't a priest live with that suffering if he knew he was helping people to have hope?

At the Sacred Hearts headquarters in Honolulu, Bishop Maigret was asking himself the same questions. For several years his priests had been insisting that someone must be sent to help the people of Molokai. Occasional visits weren't good enough.

In May 1873, the Bishop looked at the healthy, cheerful faces of four of his youngest priests, who had joined him for the dedication of a new church. He knew he could not ask one of them to move permanently to Molokai—that man would be almost certain to catch leprosy. "Could you set up some sort of rotating system?" he asked them.

The four young men agreed enthusiastically. Each would spend three months at Molokai, then go back to his own district. "I'll go first," said Damien.

Damien started immediately for Molokai. As he watched the gloomy island rising out of the dark sea, Damien wondered if this might be his new and permanent home. Even before he agreed to go to Molokai, when he said good-bye to his friends in his district, he'd had a strange feeling that he would never return.

As it turned out, Damien was right. The newspapers in Honolulu were full of the story of the brave priest who had gone to live *permanently* at Molokai. Damien had already told Bishop Maigret that he wanted to stay at Molokai. Why risk the lives of those other brave priests? the bishop wondered. Perhaps God's will was behind that mistake in the newspapers.

The Sacred Hearts Fathers decided Damien should remain on the island. For the next 16 years, except for a few short visits to Honolulu, Father Damien was shut up in the prison of Molokai.

For Damien the short journey from his landing place to Kalawao, the village where most of the patients lived, was a nightmare in real life. It was as if a graveyard had opened and decomposing bodies had risen up. Damien saw people with fingers and toes missing, huge hanging ears, noses rotting away. Person after person reached out to touch him with distorted hands or asked for his blessing on a misshapen, bloody forehead. A putrid smell hung everywhere.

Damien forced his face into a smile and steeled his body against rising nausea. "Come on, my boy," he muttered to himself. "This is your life's work."

The village he saw scarcely deserved the name. It was no more than a filthy collection of grass shacks: a strong wind would quickly knock them down, Damien thought. The only solid-looking buildings were the church and the hospital.

That night he lay under a pandanus tree and thought of the work ahead of him. He had nothing with him but his book of prayers, a cross and an extra shirt. His head ached from the sights and smells of that day. Would he ever become accustomed to them? For he must never hurt the feelings of his new parishioners. Would he catch the disease himself?

Thε people of Molokai soon decided they liked their priest. He was tough with people who wouldn't cooperate with him, but he was gentle with everyone else.

He was not like the white doctors, who were afraid to touch them and left their medicines on the top of a gate. The attendants in the hospital taught him to dress the wounds of the patients, and now he came right into their huts to tend the sick and the dying. Those patients who were close to death were covered with huge sores, which were often filled with worms eating away at their bodies. But whatever he felt, the priest never showed that he was disgusted by his patients. Sometimes he had to step outside for a few minutes because the smell was so bad. But he had begun to smoke a pipe, and the clouds of smoke around his head seemed to help.

He wasn't a great preacher, but they liked what he told them: "Earth is only a place we are passing through, an exile. Heaven is our real homeland. We lepers, we are sure of going there soon. We will be repaid for our miseries. No more hideous leprosy, no more sufferings there! We will be changed, be happier and more beautiful, the more patiently we have borne our suffering here below." He always talked about "we lepers" even though he didn't have leprosy. After all, he told them, we are all sinners and children of God.

Though only 200 of the nearly 1,000 people in the colony were Catholics, many more were soon coming to hear his message; after only three months, 400 people were studying to become members of the church. But when it came to helping people, he didn't seem to care whether they were Catholics or not. He helped everybody.

When Damien looked around Kalawao, he saw work to be done as well as souls to be saved. In fact, the two were related. Only by showing love here on earth, by devoting himself to them, could he persuade people that God loved them.

The strong wind that Damien had predicted would knock down the grass shacks soon blew. With donations from friends and money from the Hawaiian Board of Health, he began to build more solid houses for the villagers. Slowly the shacks were replaced by rows of neat white houses.

With the help of stronger patients, he laid pipes from a pool in the wilderness, so that the people had fresh water to keep themselves clean.

Clothing and food were also important in making the patients more comfortable and helping them to live longer. Damien constantly badgered the Board of Health to live up to its responsibilities. The board members grumbled that he never seemed to understand that there just wasn't enough money, but the supplies improved. Meanwhile, he stocked his own warehouse. The villagers knew that "If we need anything, *Makua Kamiano* [Father Damien] will help us."

But there was one problem he could not solve: nearly all of the people of Molokai were going to die. In a typical week, two or three people would be buried. If Damien wanted to convince his people that death was a release, he would have to take away the horror surrounding it.

One day, shortly after he arrived at Molokai, Damien watched in dismay as two men walked by, swinging a corpse tied to a pole. Damien followed them to the makeshift cemetery, where they dumped the body into a shallow grave. Scarcely had they left before wild hogs were rooting at the dirt, dragging up the pathetic body.

That night, Damien sawed and hammered in the one-room home he had built; from now on he would try to build coffins for everyone who died. From Honolulu he ordered a white picket fence and cross for a new graveyard; he made sure the graves were dug deeply. Funerals became more cheerful. Damien organized two burial societies, which competed to produce the most beautiful music and banners. The church also was vibrant with music and colour. If one of the musicians lost a finger, Damien simply replaced it with a splint.

Although Damien was sometimes impatient because change came so slowly, his superiors and the Hawaiian government were pleased with his results. Members of the royal family visited him several times and presented him with the Order of Kalakaua. The Board of Health asked for his advice, and the superintendent of the settlement, who lived on the other side of Molokai, used him as an unofficial assistant.

But not everyone was glad to have Damien on Molokai. Many patients resented him because he tried to stop the drunkenness and orgies. They never knew when a wild party would be interrupted by the stern and sturdy priest, carrying a large cane which he used vigorously when he had to.

Damien never did completely defeat this darker side of life at Molokai; after all, he was not the ruler of the colony. But there was one practice that he could do something about. Leprosy could strike the young as well as the old. In the colony there were many children who had leprosy or who had been left as orphans when their parents died. With no one to care for them, they were "adopted" by some of the most vicious adults and used as slaves or prostitutes. Father Damien and his cane put an end to that.

But what was he to do with all these children? Damien applied his usual rule: when in doubt, build. Begging money from the bishop, the Board of Health and even the wealthier members of the settlement, he built dormitories for these boys and girls. By the mid-1880s, he had 40 children living near him. There was never quite enough room, but nobody seemed to mind.

Damien always set aside a few hours a day for these children. He taught them to garden, turning the work into a game, and soon the children were growing food to eat or to sell. Those who were well enough played games and learned to cook and sew, and all studied their religion. But most of all, they loved to hear Father Damien—the only parent most of them had—read aloud the letters from his mother or brother Pamphile, now a distinguished teacher in France. Often Damien would realize with a start that he had spent the whole morning with the children. Then he would be off to visit his parishioners, care for the sick or work on one of his building projects.

Damien was still as strong as when he had arrived in the colony, but the work was exhausting. Some days he had terrible pains in his feet. One night he poured himself a bowl of hot water and began to soak his aching feet. After a few minutes he glanced down. His feet had turned scarlet, and white ribbons of skin were floating in the bowl.

The water was boiling hot, yet he had felt nothing.

A few months later, in May 1885, Dr. Arning, a world-renowned leprosy specialist, confirmed what Damien already knew. As he saw the white-coated doctor hesitate, Damien said, "Don't be afraid to tell me I have leprosy. I've been sure of it for a long time."

The doctors believed it was Damien's own fault he had caught leprosy. If he had taken a few precautions....

At first Damien had tried to be careful. But he soon realized that if he was going to help his people he would have to live freely with them. How could they believe in God's love if God's priest was afraid of them and disgusted by them? So he touched their sores, ate from the same pot, worked with the same tools and shared his pipe with them.

Some of Damien's superiors were rather relieved that he would now be confined to his prison. He was an intense, difficult man, always demanding more for his colony, as if no one else had any problems or needed money. He wasn't exactly disobedient, but he had a habit of always doing things his own way. By the time his superiors found out what he was up to, it was too late to say no. Really, they said, the man was still only a peasant, with his bursts of temper, his tactlessness and his rough sense of humour. Once when a helper commented that one of Damien's students had the catechism at his fingertips, Damien responded, "But the poor fellow has no fingertips."

Some of the people on Molokai thought that was funny, but it made the priests back in Honolulu wince.

But now that Damien himself had leprosy, the misunderstandings became worse. From that small island in the Pacific the news quickly spread. Offers of help and huge sums of money came from all around the world.

When the newspapers began to publish stories about the pitiful sufferers of Molokai and the "leper priest" who was their only support, the Board of Health was embarassed. And annoyed. So were

Damien's superiors. The publicity implied that Damien was doing the whole thing on his own, as if the government and the Sacred Hearts Fathers were doing nothing to help him.

Bishop Maigret, who had helped Damien so much during his early years, had died. The new bishop was a less sympathetic man who didn't understand Damien. He and his assistant blamed Damien for the embarassing publicity (though they never explained how a man who couldn't leave Molokai could control what newspapers around the world were publishing). After a long day's work, the dying priest, his body crippled with pain, would strain his weakened eyes to read letters from Honolulu telling him that he was disobedient, reckless, proud and selfish.

Maybe they were right, Damien would think to himself. He knew his weaknesses well. Sometimes he felt he was a failure as a priest.

What he really wanted now—what he had wanted for years—was helpers. He worked as hard as ever, but he knew that soon he would no longer be able to climb on roofs to fix leaks or work into the night making coffins. Much as he loved his children, he realized someone else would do a much better job of running the orphanage. But more than anything he wanted another priest. He had come to Molokai to help the people learn how to die. Now he was dying, and there was no one to help him, to give him the sacraments that were so important to him.

One day in July 1886 a slim, lithe man arrived at Molokai. He had read about Father Damien in a Catholic newspaper and come directly to Hawaii to help him. "Brother Joseph" was invaluable—kind, thorough, conscientious and as calm as Damien was excitable. No one ever heard him raise his voice or saw him lose his temper. Though he was already 43—only three years younger than Damien—Brother Joseph served the mission for 42 years until he died. He never contracted leprosy.

Two years later another man, "Brother James," came to help in the orphanage and to nurse Father Damien when necessary.

And finally from America the priest Damien had been waiting for arrived. Father Conrardy, a Belgian who had worked with the Indians, was the perfect companion for Damien—straightforward, devout and totally dedicated to the people of Molokai.

But one of Damien's happiest days—and also one of his saddest—came in November 1888. On that day, he took the Franciscan Sisters of Charity to meet the girls of his orphanage.

As the little girls gathered around, the priest shuffled into place and adjusted his dusty hat, its wide brim held up by pieces of string. "My children," he told them, "I shall die soon, but you shall not be abandoned. The sisters have come to care for you." The nuns, who had come all the way from America, would be taking them to a new and better home on the other side of the settlement, he explained.

But instead of smiling, the girls began to cry. Father Damien tried to explain to the children that they would be much better off with the sisters. Slowly the nuns began to lead the weeping children away. But two of them clung to the priest's battered legs. "Father, we want to stay here until your death," they said. Damien nodded.

As the children marched away, Damien thought about his years at Molokai. He knew his superiors were right. He was a rough, headstrong peasant. But if he hadn't been tough, he would never have changed the leprosy settlement from a hell to a happy and prosperous village. Now other people would correct his mistakes.

He stroked the heads of the two little girls with his knotted, clawlike hands, covered with open sores. There was no harm in keeping the two children with him. They would not long outlive him. As he looked down at their disfigured but smiling faces, he knew there was one thing he had accomplished. They would die knowing God loved them. They would know it because an ordinary priest, with a hasty temper and a talent for carpentry, had given his life to make their lives better.

In 16 years at Molokai, Damien had seen nearly 2,400 people die. Finally on April 15, 1889, it was his turn. The people of Molokai buried him under the pandanus tree where he had spent his first night in the colony.

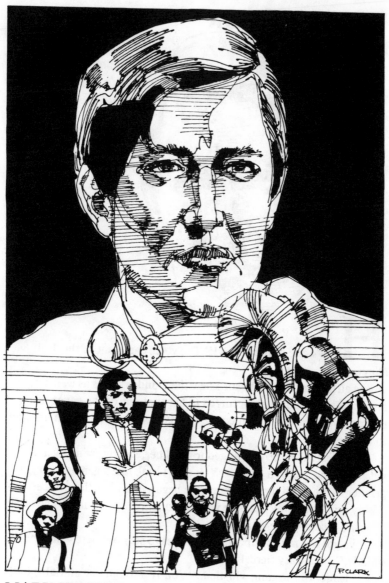

MARY SLESSOR

Deeper into the African jungle

MARY SLESSOR

Here's one o' them now!" The voice came out of the dark alleyway.

The girl froze. Mary Slessor knew the Dundee slums as well as anyone. But is had never occurred to her that one of the gangs of unemployed boys that roamed the streets would attack her on her way to the church mission.

The tallest of the boys lounged toward her, slowly swinging a heavy weight on the end of a chain. "You don't look like a gentle gospel-grinder to me, with that red hair," he began in a wheedling voice. "Why don't you stay out here with us and have some fun?" The other boys laughed and closed in.

"I've got too much important business to stay out here with a pack of kids," said Mary fiercely.

The leader of the gang whistled. "You're a tough one all right. Let's see how tough you are."

He began to swing the weight over his head. Mary could feel the wind of it ruffle her hair.

"Fine," she said, folding her arms. "But I'll expect something from you if I don't back down."

"Done!" said the boy. The weight whistled closer and closer. In a moment it would rip across her forehead. Mary stared her attacker straight in the eye. Suddenly the weight dropped.

The boy laughed admiringly. "You're tough, all right. We'll let you past now."

"That's not enough," Mary retorted. "I said I wanted a forfeit. I want all of you to come to the meeting at the mission."

A few rude noises came from the back of the crowd, but the tall boy silenced them. "Right. You won fair. We'll do what you want."

In later years, a photograph of the boy, now grown up, hung on the wall of Mary Slessor's home. He had joined the mission, found a good job and sent her the picture in gratitude for the way she'd changed his life.

But by then Mary was thousands of miles away, working with people who made the toughs of the Dundee slums seem tame.

If the gang had known more about Mary and her family, they wouldn't have been surprised at her courage. Mary was tough, because she had lived a tough life. Like most children in the industrial cities of Britain in the mid-19th century, she had gone to work in the mills when she was 11, working from six in the morning till six at night. On Saturday nights, in the one-room house in Dundee, Scotland, where she lived with her parents and brothers and sisters, she and her mother would sit by the fire watching her father's dinner slowly dry to a crust. Late at night, he returned, sometimes singing, sometimes cursing. Mary's mother kept quiet, but Mary wouldn't back down from her father's drunken insults. At times she could dodge his fists until he passed out on the floor. But other times she wasn't quick enough. With her head still ringing, her bare feet cold on the pavement, she'd wait outside the door, keeping an eye out for other drunks stumbling home until her mother could let her back in.

The only relief came on Sunday, when her mother took them to church. That was a different world—clean, quiet, where people were kind to each other. The family particularly loved to hear about the far-off mission of Calabar in Africa with its lush green jungles.

When her father died, it was almost a relief for Mary. Now she was the family's chief breadwinner.

Meanwhile, at the mills she had been promoted. She was also teaching Sunday school classes and, through the mission, helping other people who lived in the slums with their problems of alcoholism and poverty. And in every spare moment, there was reading and studying. Her employers even allowed her to keep a book by her loom.

But sometimes she still dreamed about green forests and black children.

By 1875, both her brothers were dead. Her mother and sisters depended on Mary's salary, but she decided she could earn as much by being what she had always wanted to be: a missionary.

That year, Mary Slessor was accepted as a missionary to Calabar by her church's Foreign Missions' Board.

The slave trade was almost as bad for the Africans who were left behind as it was for those who were carried off as slaves. As well as paying Africans to capture other Africans as slaves, the traders encouraged violence and heavy drinking. The old tribal systems of law and order were destroyed. Protestant missionaries had been comimg to Calabar, on the coast of what is now Nigeria, since 1846 to try to help the natives by teaching them "God" (Christian beliefs) and "Book" (how to read and write). But so far they had only been successful with the Efik, who lived at the mouth of the Cross River.

Farther up the river, the Okoyong still followed the old ways, murdering slaves and relatives when someone important died and going on wild drinking binges. When the Okoyong villages were not warring with other tribes, such as the Efik, they fought among themselves.

For 12 years, Mary worked patiently for the mission at Calabar as a teacher and nurse, learning the language, customs and religion of the Efik natives.

To the surprise of some other missionaries, she adopted African ways, discarding the heavy petticoats of a Victorian lady for a simple cotton smock, cutting her long hair, eating local food, sleeping on hard clay benches and walking far into the jungle. Her tough childhood in the slums had been good training.

Then, in 1886, news came from home. Her mother and remaining sister were now dead. There was no one back in Scotland to worry about her.

At last she felt free to fulfill her ambition, to go deeper into the jungle to work with the Okoyong.

By the time the canoe bearing Mary and the five orphans she had adopted neared the Okoyong village at Ekenge, where Chief Edem had invited her to stay, it was night. The Efik guides were terrified of walking into the strange village, so Mary and the children went on alone through the darkness.

But when they got to the village, it was deserted. In the distance, Mary could hear shouting and gunshots. An old slave woman explained that the mother of the chief in the neighbouring village had died, and the people of Ekenge had gone to share in the bloody, drunken funeral rites.

It was several days before Chief Edem and his people came back to the village. His wives told Mary that it had been a grand funeral: 24 people had been killed and buried with the chief's mother to serve as her slaves in the next world, and four people suspected of killing her by witchcraft had taken a trial by poison and died.

"The tribe seemed so completely given over to the devil," Mary wrote to her friends in Calabar, "that we were tempted to despair."

Yet there were encouraging signs. The Okoyong, slave and free, were eager to learn. Before long, many knew the Efik alphabet and could do simple sums. They were also grateful to her for the medical treatment she gave them. They even came to Sunday services, learning the words of hymns that Mary set to popular Scottish songs.

And she had made a friend. Most Okoyong women were considered little better than goods, to be traded or even destroyed at their husbands' wish. But Chief Edem's sister, Eme, had great influence over him. She was anxious to help Mary in her attempts at reform. They agreed that whenever there was trouble, Eme would send Mary an empty gin bottle with a note asking for medicine. The villagers were amazed that the "white Ma" always seemed to know when they were up to something.

Mary began to like these people, despite their violent life. In many ways she was like them. She could be tough, even though she was afraid of many things in the jungle. She shared their love of fun. She even admired some things about their religion. They were not like Europeans, who could turn their religion on or off. To the Okoyong, the world was full of gods and spirits who had to be constantly appeased. Over all was one mighty god, Abassi.

If only she could convince them that God was loving and kind, not vengeful and cruel, their whole way of life could be changed.

Mary knew she would have to be careful. Unlike the Efik, these people had not yet learned to respect her. If she offended them, they could send her back to Calabar. Or, even more likely, they could murder her and tell the mission she had been killed by some jungle animal.

Then an incident happened that made red-headed Mary forget her good resolutions.

One evening Mary saw the villagers gathering in the marketplace, bringing drums and crates of gin. A man had asked another man's slave to do work for him, Eme explained. While the employer was away, the slave demanded his payment of yams from the man's wife. When she refused, he threatened her. Finally, she gave him a piece of yam, promising to pay the rest later. For this she was to be punished by having boiling oil poured over her belly.

Mary was horrified. "But why?"

"Food is the source of all life, Ma. It is the wife's duty to offer it to her husband. If she offers it to another man, it means that she offers him herself. She is committing adultery. Perhaps it doesn't make sense to you, but the Egbo Council has decided. It would be dangerous to try to stop them."

Above the drums and drunken laughter, Mary could hear screaming. She knew Eme was right about the danger. The secret Egbo Council, composed of the elders of many villages, relied on terror to impose its justice.

But Mary was furious and couldn't stop herself. She ran to the marketplace and pushed her way through the crowd. In the flicker of the torches, she could see masked men tying a naked, writhing woman to the ground. Another masked man stood by the fire, ladling bubbling palm oil into a pot.

Mary sprang at the men tying the woman and began to slap and poke them. "Stop that at once!" she ordered.

The crowd gasped. Did the white woman really believe she could stop the power of Egbo?

Mary turned to face the chief torturer. "Put that down."

The man began to move toward her, his body quivering with

feathers and fur, the firelight bouncing off the bits of tin that covered his body. If he attacked her, the whole crowd would burst into a bloody, drunken riot.

He began to swing the ladle over his head. The swooshing metal came closer and closer.

A memory flickered across her mind. Suddenly Mary knew how to handle this situation. Crossing her arms, she glared at the Egbo man insolently. He stopped. She took a step forward, then another. The torturer stumbled and fell as he tried to back away. The crowd, which a moment before had been ready to rip her to pieces, began to laugh.

Mary half-carried the frightened woman back to her hut and tended to her wounds. When Mary finally went to bed, she couldn't sleep for happiness and wonder. Her temper had driven her to take a foolish risk. Yet God had protected her!

In the morning, she discovered that the villagers had come to the same conclusion. Only a woman who was truly favored by God would have dared to oppose the Egbo. So Ma must have a very great magic indeed. From that day on, Mary had an unprecedented power over the tribes. And she used it!

But even though Mary was successful in persuading them to drop many of their violent customs, the Okoyong still insisted on an orgy of killing every time an important person died. One day Mary and Charles Ovens, a world traveller who had read about Mary and come from Scotland to help her build her house, heard a mournful cry from the forest. Etim, the chief's eldest son, had been struck by a falling log. A few days later he died.

Mary went into action. She washed Etim's body and dressed it in a white shirt and dark suit, with a length of fine silk around the waist. She wrapped another piece of silk around the head and crowned it with a top hat. Then she painted the face bright yellow, an honor reserved for the mightiest chiefs.

"What on earth are you doing?" asked the astonished Ovens.

Mary explained that she was trying to make Etim's burial as grand as possible, so that he would not need a retinue of followers to go with him to the spirit world.

When the villagers saw the corpse, they were impressed. But Chief Edem was not satisfied. That night, Charles Ovens left the village with an urgent message for the mission at Calabar.

Meanwhile, warriors had brought 12 prisoners from a neighboring village, accusing them of killing Etim by witchcraft. To prove their innocence, the captives would be forced to take the bean test. Anyone who drank the milky liquid and survived was innocent. But since the bean was poison, few survived.

Mary confronted Edem. "You know that this test does not work. If you took it, you too would die. Does that mean you also are guilty of killing your son?"

Edem was as drunk as he was grief-stricken. And he was furious with Mary for ruining his son's funeral. But finally, he and the visiting chiefs agreed to let the suspects take an oath. Although this was considered to be even greater magic than the bean test, it was harmless.

All passed until they got to the final prisoner. Then Edem roared, "Not her! My son must have at least one slave to follow him to the spirit world." Chiefs and warriors shouted their agreement. Once again it seemed certain that Mary would be attacked by the mob.

Suddenly Eme went on her knees before her brother. "If you carry on like this, the white Ma will go to another village, and you will no

longer be the greatest chief," she whispered frantically in his ear. "Let
the slave woman be chained in Mary's yard until you make a
decision."

Edem agreed.

The next day, two missionaries arrived from Calabar with Mary's
solution to the problem: a projector and slides. "This is done in honor
of Edem, so that those in the spirit world will know he is a great
man," she announced. The village was astounded by the pictures of
the white man's world. All agreed that no man had ever had such a
funeral. Etim went to his grave with no murdered slaves to accompany
him, the first time this had happened among the Okoyong.

Now it seemed that almost every week a delegation arrived to
ask Mary to bring God and Book to a new village. Mary would set off,
walking through the endless wet, clinging undergrowth to visit these
tribespeople, giving them medicine, founding schools and conducting
worship services.

The journeys were hard, lonely and dangerous. As well as hostile
warriors, the jungle was full of dangerous animals. Once Mary
frightened away a leopard by singing to it. "My singing would scare
any decent, respectable leopard," she wrote to her friends.

Another time she was being paddled down to headquarters in
Calabar for medical treatment when her canoe was attacked by a huge
hippo. When the panic-stricken boatmen failed to drive it off, Mary
hit it on the snout with a pole and shouted, "Go away you!" The star-
tled beast did just that.

She was just as courageous and blunt in dealing with troublesome
humans. Once, when two villages were about to go to war, they found
the white Ma already on the battlefield. Standing between the two
tribes, she dared them to shoot. Then she commanded them to turn
their guns over to her. The tribesmen humbly dropped their weapons
in front of the tiny Scot and returned home.

Not everyone appreciated Mary's way of dealing with the
Africans. Some of the more proper whites were disgusted by the way
she had "gone native." Mary only replied impatiently, "How can I
learn to think like them if I don't live the way they do?"

When she was in Calabar she enjoyed shocking the starchy visitors.

Once, a female journalist asked to talk to her. Mary agreed, but there was a gleam in her eye. The journalist later reported to her readers that Mary Slessor was indeed an admirable character but that she had no idea how to dress herself. Mary had come to the interview wearing a wild collection of second-hand clothes topped by a big, battered green hat with a red bow!

Mary rarely took vacations, because there was no one to take her place with the Okoyong while she was gone. But every few years she became so ill from malaria that even she realized she needed a rest.

During her trips back to Scotland—which could last more than a year, depending on how sick she was—she went on speaking tours, often taking along one of the black children she had adopted. As a result, her work became famous. More and more people sent her letters and money. But the new missionaries she needed to continue her work never came. Instead, she began to train Africans to conduct their own services and to teach lessons.

And still Mary wanted to move farther into the jungle.

Meanwhile, the British government was also penetrating deeper into Africa, trying to open up trade and stop warfare. Everywhere they went, the people told them about *Eda Kpukpro Owo,* the Mother of All the Peoples. With her knowledge of African ways and her hold over the people, Mary was an obvious person to become one of the judges in the newly opened territories. Thus, in 1891 at the age of 43, Mary Slessor became the first woman Vice-Consul in the British Empire.

Mary's way of holding court was effective, if unusual. The British sent their rookie officials to observe Mary so that they could learn about native customs and attitudes. One of these novices described her methods in court, where she presided in a rocking chair with a baby in her lap: "Suddenly she jumped up with an angry growl, her shawl fell off, the baby was hurriedly transferred to somebody qualified to hold it, and with a few trenchant words she made for the door where a hulking overdressed native stood. In a moment she seized him by the scruff of the neck, boxed his ear and hustled him into the yard telling him quite explicitly what would happen to him if he came back again without her consent.... Then as suddenly as it had arisen the tornado subsided, and (lace shawl, baby and all) she was gently swaying in her chair again.''

The man had been rude to her, and she had forbidden him to come back until he apologized.

No one could deny that she had amazing success. In the villages where she worked, funeral killings and the trial by poison bean were almost completely wiped out. The tribes were trading with each other and with whites and learning to settle their differences through the courts rather than in battle. Drunkenness was still a problem, but mainly among the men. The women and children no longer took part in the binges. And because of Mary, the men were beginning to have greater respect for their women. Mary had shown that a woman could be an important and useful person.

Converting the Africans to Christian beliefs was more difficult; even her friend Eme still worshipped the old gods. But the natives were building churches, and many had become staunch Christians even though they were sometimes persecuted by their tribes.

In 1913, a message came for her. King George had sent Mary the silver cross of the Order of St. John. She was ordered to come down the river to Calabar to receive it.

Such public appearances were agony to Mary. Once, when she was speaking to a large crowd in Scotland, she had lost her nerve and run from the platform. But she couldn't disobey.

Mary was no longer strong and healthy. When she arrived in Calabar, her friends were not surprised at her appearance—doctors had told her many times that she could not survive the harsh life of the jungle much longer. Constant fevers, rough travel and lack of proper food had worn her down. Now in her sixties, she was crippled by rheumatism. For a while, she had ridden a bicycle; then it had been replaced by a wheelchair. Other times, her devoted followers carried her through the jungle. When she had to travel by canoe, she often took a heavy dose of laudanum for her pain and curled up to sleep on the bottom of the canoe.

But she felt fine for the celebrations. There was a tea party and a cricket match in her honor. And there was the presentation of the St. John's cross. All through the speeches, she sat with her head in her hands, embarrassed by the praise and thinking of the miraculous protection that seemed to have been over her all the time she had lived in the jungle.

When she rose to speak—partly in English, partly in Efik—she told the crowd, "If I have done anything in my life, it has been easy because the Master has gone before."

As the boat carried her back to the jungle, the other missionaries watched the small, wizened figure and wondered if she would ever come back. They had wondered the same thing 25 years before, when she first left to live with the Okoyong.

This time she didn't come back. In their last sight of Mary, she was staring straight ahead, clutching a huge bouquet of roses. A year and a half later she died at 66, after 38 years as a missionary.

There was still much work to be done and never enough people to do it. A band of devoted followers, including some of the children she adopted, continued her work, but it was a tough mission, with little support from home.

Mary loved roses. When the bouquet her friends had given her began to fade, she planted the roses in her garden. One took root and blossomed, a sweet and strange presence in the jungle, in the same way that a Scottish girl's faith took root in African life and began to change it.

HARRIET TUBMAN

Bound for the promised land

HARRIET TUBMAN

Twelve thousand dollars is a lot of money for a slave woman!'' said the tall man with the cigar, staring in amazement at the boldly lettered poster that announced the reward for capturing Harriet Tubman.

His companion scowled. "Not when you think of what she's been doing to the farmers here in Maryland. We've lost more than 60 slaves in the past month. Burning alive's too good for her."

The tall man tapped his friend on the shoulder and nodded toward a stocky black woman sitting on a bench farther down the railway platform. "Maybe that's her right there." In her mission to rescue the slaves of the South, Harriet Tubman could appear anywhere at any time.

As they watched, the woman took a book out of her carpet bag and opened it. "No, that can't be her," said the shorter man. "The one we want can't read."

As the two men strolled by, Harriet fixed her eyes on the page before her and devoutly hoped the book was right side up.

Harriet had never been a "good" slave. Her parents knew that working in the master's mansion was an easier life than field labour, so they were delighted when she became a housemaid. But Harriet could never please her mistress. When she was seven, after working all day she was expected to sit up through the night nursing a sick baby. If she dropped off for a moment, the baby would cry, and Harriet would be whipped. The scars on her face and neck remained all her life.

By the time she was 12, her master had given up. From now on Harriet would work in the fields. Though only five feet tall, she became as strong as any of the men. One of the overseers brought his friends to show them this female wonder, lifting huge barrels and pulling heavy carts like an ox. The overseers valued her for her strength; they were even a little afraid of her, for she didn't keep silent like the other slaves. If anyone, black or white, spoke sharply to her, she snapped right back at him.

One fall evening, when Harriet was still in her early teens, the overseer noticed that one slave was missing. Someone said he had gone to the village store. Seizing his whip, the overseer set off across the fields—with Harriet following. The missing slave might be trying to escape, and she wanted to be there to make sure no harm came to him.

By the time the overseer got to the store, he was furious. "I'll whip your hide off," he screamed at the black slave. "Tie him down." Nobody moved—except the frightened slave, who made for the door. Harriet, who had watched everything, quickly blocked the door after him. Grabbing a heavy weight from the counter, the overseer hurled it after the fleeing slave. The weight hit Harriet on the temple.

It was months before she recovered. The blow left a huge dint in her forehead, and she began to have sleeping spells. In the middle of sweeping or working in the fields, she would suddenly fall asleep wherever she stood, then wake after a few minutes and continue whatever she was doing.

Her master believed she had become feeble-minded, and Harriet encouraged that belief. No one wanted to buy a slow-witted slave. Harriet was afraid of being sold farther south, where the slave-owners were even more brutal and she would be farther from the Mason-Dixon line, the border that separated the slave-owning Southern states from the Northern free states.

For Harriet had decided that, more than anything, she wanted to be free. Sometimes at night with the other slaves she would steal away to the backwoods to listen to someone read the Bible and to sing of the "sweet chariot" that would carry them across the Jordan to a new home. God had promised them heaven, Harriet knew, but she also believed that God had created all people equal and equally free. Black people shouldn't have to wait till they were dead to be free.

One Saturday night in 1849, a rumour raced through the slave quarters: two of Harriet's sisters had been taken away to be sold in the deep South, and more slaves would be sold. Harriet persuaded three of her brothers to make a run for freedom with her. Afraid of the hundreds of people in the area who knew them and could betray them, of the bloodhounds that would follow and drag them down, of the cut of the whip, Harriet's brothers turned back. Though she pleaded with them, they forced Harriet to return, too.

The rumours grew stronger. Harriet waited anxiously through Sunday, then Monday, certain that at any moment the men would come to take her away. On Monday night, another slave crept to her cabin; he had heard for sure that Harriet and her brothers would be taken away that very night.

This time she was going alone. She would tell no one her plans, except her sister Mary. Harriet went to the kitchen of the master's house, where Mary worked. Sneaking up behind her, Harriet gave her sister a shove. Laughing and gasping for breath, Mary chased Harriet out into the yard. Suddenly, both girls stopped short. The master, Doctor Thompson, was sitting on his horse by the gate. Mary quickly darted back into the kitchen. Harriet stood for a moment, then began to sing, loud enough for her sister to hear. She walked calmly by the Doctor, hoping he wouldn't guess the meaning of the hymn she sang:

"*I'll meet you in the morning,*
I'm bound for the promised land,
On the other side of Jordan,
Bound for the promised land."

Mary, standing by the window, guessed where the promised land was; to the Doctor, it was only a hope for the hereafter. What right did any slave have to wish for a better life on earth?

A white woman who lived nearby had already given Harriet the names of people who would help her on her journey, conductors on the "Underground Railroad" who had already helped hundreds of slaves to escape from the South. It wasn't really a railroad at all, just a

network of people. But they were so efficient at helping slaves escape
that some slave owners thought there must be trains whisking their
slaves away!

Creeping slowly through the woods, avoiding the main roads,
Harriet came to the first house or "station" on her list.

Instead of hiding her, the woman shoved a broom at her. "Start
sweeping," she said. Harriet worked in the front yard till the evening,
as far as anyone could see a dedicated slave cleaning up for her
mistress. When the woman's husband came home, he hid her in his
cart and drove her to the next station. From there, Harriet continued
her journey, sometimes hiding with white families, sometimes sleeping
in the woods, but always heading north.

Finally, early one morning, she crossed into the free state of Penn-
sylvania. "When I found I had crossed that line," she said later, "I
looked at my hands to see if I was the same person. There was such a
glory over everything; the sun came like gold through the trees and
over the fields, and I felt like I was in heaven."

Harriet had no education, but she knew how to work, and she
was soon able to support herself, cooking, cleaning and doing laundry
in hotels. But though freedom was wonderful, it was also lonely. She
felt like a man who had just been released from jail after 25 years and
finds his home, family and friends all gone. "I was free, but there was
no one to welcome me to the land of freedom. I was a stranger in a
strange land, and my home, after all, was down in Maryland, because
my father, my mother, my brothers, and sisters, and friends were
there. But I was free, and they should be free. I would make a home in
the North and bring them there, God helping me. Oh, how I prayed
then. I said to the Lord, 'I'm going to hold steady on to you, and I
know you'll see me through.'"

She began to get in touch with the abolitionists, white and black
people who were working in many different ways for the end of
slavery. She told them she was going back. Her friends tried to talk
her out of it. There was worthwhile work she could do in the free
states. Working on the Underground Railroad was dangerous enough,
even for whites, but as a black woman who could neither read nor
write and who might be recognized by the local people, she would be

much more vulnerable.

Harriet wouldn't listen. She may never have read the Bible, but she had a strong faith. "There's two things I've got a right to," she told her abolitionist friends, "and these are death or liberty—one or the other I mean to have. No one will take me back alive; I shall fight for my liberty, and when the time has come for me to go, the Lord will let them kill me."

Back in Maryland, Harriet's sister Mary and her two children were to be sold away from the plantation. On the morning of the auction, Mary's husband, a free black man, waited anxiously. By noon, Mary had not yet been sold. The auctioneer went for lunch. When he came back, Mary and her children were gone.

A few days later, a black family cautiously approached a house in Baltimore, Maryland. The door was opened by Harriet. Mary and her children—and several other slaves whom Harriet had persuaded to run for freedom—were soon on board the first Underground Railroad trip conducted by Harriet Tubman.

There would be 18 more trips. By the time the Civil War broke out, Harriet had personally conducted about 300 slaves to freedom and had inspired hundreds more to flee. Although she couldn't read or write, although sudden sleeping spells would overtake her in the middle of a journey, and although large rewards were posted for her capture, she was never caught.

Harriet had the genius of a great general for planning and leading. Before each journey she would save her money to buy food for the trip and to bribe people to help her.

Soon after she had saved enough money, the word would go round the slave quarters of some Southern plantation that "Moses" had come to lead them out of Egypt to freedom. In the middle of the night slaves crept away from their cabins to make escape plans with Harriet in the woods. She took only those she believed had the strength of will to finish the journey.

The next Saturday night they would leave. No advertisements for their capture could be posted on Sunday, so they had one clear day. They would escape along one of the multitude of routes that Harriet now knew, sleeping in the woods or in the cellars, attics and barns of white friends along the way.

The trip was long and rough. One time she hid with a group of 25 slaves in a swamp all day without food. When it was finally safe to move, one of the men refused to go on. They were all going to die anyway, he said, and at least he could die at home.

Harriet knew that if he went back, they would probably all be caught. Suddenly the man heard a click and felt the cold steel of a pistol at his temple.

"Move or die!" said Harriet.

He moved.

Harriet's plans were daring. Often the slaves would steal their master's horse and carriage and drive for the first stage of the journey. Anyone seeing them would assume that they were on some errand; no slave would dare escape by the open road in daylight. By the time the advertisements were put up, the slaves would be far away.

Sometimes if Harriet realized that they were under suspicion, they would simply take the train *south;* everyone expected that fugitive slaves would always head north.

Sometimes disguises were used. Once Harriet had to enter a village where one of her former overseers lived. She hunched her back and tottered along like an old woman, carrying a bunch of live chickens by a string tied around their legs. As she turned a corner, she suddenly saw her old overseer. Quickly she cut the cord. The villagers laughed at the sight of the old woman scurrying after her squawking fowl. The overseer passed by without even recognizing his former slave.

There were other close escapes. One time, Harriet's friends found her fast asleep in a park, beneath a poster advertising a reward for her capture. But she was always confident that God was leading her: "I always told him, 'I trust you. I don't know where to go or what to do, but I expect you to lead me,' and he always did."

Harriet was determined to rescue more of her large family. In 1854 she sent a secret message to three of her brothers, telling them "when the good old ship of Zion comes along, be ready to step aboard." She was just in time. It was Christmas Eve, a Saturday, and her brothers were to be sold on the Monday.

They met in a barn beside their parents' cabin. Through the window they could see their mother making Christmas dinner, wondering what was keeping her sons so long. But they knew this was one Christmas dinner they would have to miss; their mother was easily excited and would give them away if she heard of their plans.

Harriet's father Ben could be trusted, however. All through Christmas day, as they waited for the rain to stop, Ben made secret trips to the barn, dropping off provisions but never seeing his children. Finally night came. The four children watched for a few minutes through the window of the cabin, where their mother, her head in her hand, sat in a rocking chair by the fire, worrying over what had become of her sons. Harriet had not seen her mother in five years, yet she waited silently, making no move to enter the cabin.

Old Ben came with them on the first part of the journey but insisted on tying a blindfold around his eyes. After saying good-bye to their father, the group travelled by foot to the home of the Quaker Thomas Garrett and from there to freedom. A few days later, the slave-hunters came looking for the three vanished men. But they soon realized they

were on the wrong track. Old Ben had such a great reputation for
honesty that they knew they could believe him when he said he hadn't
seen any of his children that Christmas.

Harriet wanted to take her parents as well, but they were now nearly
70, and few older people were strong enough to survive the rough
journey to freedom. But three years later, Harriet heard news that
gave her no choice. A slave who had started to escape and then turned
back told his wife that old Ben had helped him. The wife then
betrayed Ben to the master. Ben was to be tried and would surely be
convicted. Harriet decided "to save them the expense of a trial and
remove my father to a higher court."

But first she needed money. She marched into the abolition office in
New York and demanded $20, a large sum of money at that time. The
abolitionists were sympathetic, but they didn't have that much money.
"I'm not going till I get my twenty dollars," she said and sat down to
wait. She waited all morning and all afternoon, often falling into her
sleeping fits. As she slept, the story of her problem went around, and
by the time she left, she had $60 in her pocket.

She then swooped down to Maryland and carried her parents off in
a horse and cart, again with the help of William Garrett.

The rescue enraged Southern slave-owners. Only a few weeks before
a black minister had been sentenced to 10 years in prison for having a
copy of *Uncle Tom's Cabin,* the antislavery novel by Harriet Beecher
Stowe. The slave-owners of Maryland were infuriated by the large
numbers of slaves who were escaping and the criticism of the
abolitionists in the North.

Meanwhile, people in the North were increasingly resentful
over slavery. One of the things that angered them most was the Fugitive
Slave Law. Under this law, Southerners could come into the free states
to recapture their slaves, and white residents of those states were
obliged to help them. It was bad enough to have slavery in their country at all, many Northerners felt. Now they had to help enforce it.

The Fugitive Slave Law caused a riot in Troy, New York, on April
27, 1860. Harriet was visiting a cousin when she heard that a young
black man named Charles Nalle was about to be transported back to

Virginia. Spreading the news as she went, Harriet headed for the courthouse. There she pushed her way through the huge crowd that was already gathering.

In an upstairs room, Nalle's case was being heard. The judge and policemen were alarmed by the crowd, but under the present law they had little choice but to let Nalle's accuser take him back to slavery.

When the police led Nalle down to the street, Harriet locked her arms fiercely about the captive and began to tear him away from the guards. "Drag us out!" she cried. "Drag him to the river! Drown him, but don't let them have him!" The officers clubbed the two ex-slaves repeatedly on their heads, but gradually the surging crowd carried them toward the river. By the time they got there, Nalle was barely conscious.

The crowd shoved Nalle into a rowboat. But the police were waiting on the other side. Again the fugitive was carried off to an upper room. This time his defenders rushed up the stairs and began to hurl stones at the door. Finally one man managed to drag the door open. He was immediately felled by an officer wielding an axe. But the fight was already over. Led by Harriet, a group of women swarmed into the room, seized Nalle and carried him off. Within a few minutes he was on his way to Canada, where no law could reclaim him, and Harriet was swallowed up into the underground again.

Despite the fighting spirit she showed at Troy, her friends thought of Harriet as a gentle and kindly person. She understood the slave-owners and even had compassion for them. She explained to her white friends in the North that, "They don't know any better; it's the way they were brought up."

But just as she felt she sometimes had to use the threat of violence to keep her fugitives faithful on their journey, she believed that in the end slavery would only be ended through war. She knew that slavery was "the next thing to hell" and she believed that it was justifiable to use violence to end it. She supported John Brown (the hero of the song "John Brown's Body" who tried to start a slave revolution by capturing Harper's Ferry) when he took up arms against the government and would have aided him in his raid if she hadn't been ill at the time.

When the Civil War finally came in 1861, Harriet was eager to help. The army was just as eager to have her. As they invaded the South, the soldiers were setting slaves free. Cut loose from their masters by these strange Yankees, many slaves didn't know whom to trust. The army wasn't quite sure what to do with them either. Harriet was the perfect mediator between the two groups.

At first she worked mainly as a nurse. But officers realized that Harriet's colour and talents suited her for much more dangerous work. As a Negro, she could pass behind enemy lines without comment, and her experience as a conductor on the Underground Railroad made her an excellent scout and spy.

By 1863 she was in charge of a corps of nine black scouts who reported on the movements and weaknesses of the enemy and who guided the Northern commanders on their raids. Harriet herself led and organized at least one raid, inflicting severe damage on the enemy's supplies and carrying off nearly 800 slaves without even an injury to her 300 soldiers. The commanders who used her services found her invaluable and said so often. General Saxton, one of the men she worked with, testified to her "remarkable courage, zeal and fidelity."

In 1865 the war was over, and the slaves of the South were free. It was a time for the abolitionists to congratulate themselves. Harriet was called "the heroine of the age" for her part in the war and the Underground Railroad. But she knew it was too soon to celebrate victory for the black people of America. On her way home to Auburn, New York, Harriet carried a half-fare pass as an Army employee. When the conductor on one of the trains saw the pass he refused to accept it and tried to push her off the train. With cries of "Pitch the nigger out!" three men came to his aid, and Harriet was left by the side of the tracks with her pass and a badly wrenched arm.

It was obvious to her that the fight for freedom was not over. By now she was 55, and the rest of her life would be spent helping every black person who came in trouble to her door and trying, with the help of her many admirers, to get the government to grant her the army pension she was entitled to. Finally in 1899 she got it and lived another 14 years to be 93.

Harriet was right when she said the fight was not over. For another

100 years the blacks of America would suffer a new persecution, more subtle than the old, in both North and South. Legally, they had won their freedom. In practice, they were still the victims of society. In the struggle to win the vote, better education and an end to segregation, they looked to "Moses," the conductor of the Underground Railroad, to understand what it meant to have faith and courage.

ERIC LIDDELL

The man who didn't like to be beaten

ERIC LIDDELL

TRAITOR TO HIS KING AND COUNTRY, the headlines announced. Who was the man? An officer who had deserted his troops in battle? A spy who had sold secrets to the enemy?

Eric Liddell didn't look like a traitor. He was a quiet-spoken, 22-year-old science student, with a sparkle in his eyes and a spring in his step—and with Scotland's fastest running times. His crime? He had refused to run in an Olympic race being held on a Sunday.

On a cold foggy day in April 1923, a young man named Thompson—"D.P." to his friends—trudged up the steep, grey streets of Edinburgh and rapped on the door of the Edinburgh Medical Mission Hostel. It had been a long trip from Glasgow, where he was a theological student. He wasn't even sure that he would get what he came for.

A few minutes later, a slight, wiry man walked into the living room—Eric Liddell, who many thought was Scotland's greatest athlete.

D.P. explained that the Glasgow Students' Evangelical Union wanted Eric to speak at one of their meetings: "How else can we reach men who think Christianity is a lot of mush, something real men don't believe in?''

Eric grinned. "You mean you want me to be your 'real man.' One of those 'muscular Christians'?''

"If you agree to speak, a lot of people will come who wouldn't otherwise.''

Eric dropped his head for a moment. Then he looked up. "All right. I'll come.''

Eric was not a natural orator. He was quiet and hated speaking to large groups. And even though his parents were missionaries in China, he had never said publicly that he was a Christian.

But there was something so direct and sincere about him that everyone remembered what he said. Newspapers carried his speeches. More and more people came to see him. From being a "silent disciple" he became a powerful voice for Christianity. D.P. Thompson estimated that about 200 people became ministers as a result of their campaigns, while many others became missionaries. And Eric found that his own life was changing.

For one thing, his running times kept improving. His style was still terrible. He flailed his arms and threw his head back so that he couldn't see where he was going. Once he ran straight into a photographer who had unwisely set his tripod up on the track.

People began to notice that he had a special determination. During one race, he was knocked off the track, and by the time he picked himself up the other runners were well ahead. But he caught up and won the race.

Yet when people suggested that he had a special inspiration, he just laughed. "The reason I win," he said, "is that I don't like to be beaten."

Soon it was clear that Eric Liddell would run for Britain in the 1924 Olympics. He was chosen for four races, including the 200 metres and two relay races. But the most attention was on his entry in the 100 metres. This was considered the most important race in the Olympics, and Britain had never won it.

Then the timetables came out. The trials or "heats" for the 100 metres were on Sunday.

Eric Liddell announced that he wouldn't run on a Sunday.

The press ranted. The officials of the British Olympic team railed. Even the Prince of Wales let it be known that he would be very pleased if Mr. Liddell would change his mind.

But Eric knew he had no choice. Keeping Sunday free from the activities that occupied the rest of the week was important to the Scots in the early part of this century—and is still important to many Christians today. Eric Liddell had been brought up to believe that this was part of showing respect for God. Today, a Christian athlete might face different choices—whether to play in countries that have racist laws, for example.

Eric Liddell felt he must stand by his principle, that it was better to honour God than to win a race, no matter how important. The public, the press and the officials could fuss as much as they liked; Eric Liddell wouldn't change his mind.

Eventually, the Olympic Committee told him to run in the 400 metres instead of the 100. They didn't have much hope, though. Eric had little training in the longer distance. His best effort in practice, 48.2 seconds, was well behind the record-breaking 47.8 of the American runner Horatio Fitch.

On the day of the 400 metres, the British sadly admitted they hadn't a chance.

The six finalists settled back on their starting blocks. At the sound of the pistol, they sprang forward.

Eric's inexperience showed right away. In the outside lane, he couldn't see how fast the other runners were going. He shot through the first 200 metres at a blistering pace that he couldn't possibly keep up. By the time they rounded the bend, Fitch, the American record holder, was gaining rapidly. Soon he was only two metres behind the exhausted Scot.

Then, in his famous gesture, Eric threw his head back. Running blindly, arms flailing, he actually increased his lead. He burst through the finishing tape five metres ahead of Fitch.

The crowd leaped to its feet, yelling with delight, while the announcer struggled to tell them that Eric Liddell had set a world's record, 47.6 seconds. All the talk about traitor was forgotten as Union Jacks sprang up all over the stadium.

Eric smiled as he thought of the note a friend had sent him that morning: "In the old book it says, 'He that honours me, I will honour.'"

After the noise and the ceremonies were over, friends and reporters rushed to the dressing rooms to congratulate Eric, but he was nowhere to be found. He had to preach a sermon on Sunday, and had slipped away to prepare it.

A year later, in 1925, Eric Liddell was on the Trans-Siberian Railway on his way to China, where he had been born.

There had never been any doubt in his mind that he would go back to China. Some people thought that with his athletic talent, he should pursue a running career or at least take a well-paid post at an important college. But Eric knew that there was more to life than winning races, more to honouring God than listening to the cheers of the crowd or drawing a big salary.

Eric's father had sent him reports from Tientsin, the northern city where he had been posted by the London Missionary Society. He smiled grimly as he read of famine, floods, strikes and violence.

For over a century, China had been exploited by the various European nations. As a result, many Chinese were coming to hate everything foreign—even the missionaries. They saw Christianity as part of the foreign exploitation of the country.

The Chinese politicians were divided between the Nationalists, who wanted a stronger central government, and the Communists, who wanted to change society completely. But most ordinary Chinese spent their time trying to survive natural disasters, the wandering gangs of bandits, and the Japanese, who were taking over the fringes of the country.

Despite these problems, the next few years were happy ones for Eric Liddell. He was back with his family and childhood friends. He taught science and a few English classes and was responsible for the sports program. There were Bible classes to lead, meetings to attend, games to referee.

In the summers there was vacation time at Pei-tai-ho, where many foreigners had cottages and beaches.

The community at Pei-tai-ho soon learned what Eric's friends already knew: there was a lot of mischief behind those innocent blue eyes. He once outraged the missionaries by conducting a church service on a particularly hot Sunday in his shorts. Another time a Canadian family, the Mackenzies, gave a swimming party for their friends. Everyone said that it was too bad that there was no raft in the Mackenzies' bay; there was nowhere to swim to. On the day of the party, a raft magically appeared, just like the one the Americans had at their beach. The next day the raft was gone again. It wasn't until later that the Mackenzies learned that Eric had bribed two boatmen to borrow the Americans' raft in the middle of the night and return it the next evening.

Still later, the Mackenzies learned why Eric had become such a close friend: he wanted to marry their daughter, Florence. Even Florence didn't suspect that Eric, 10 years her senior, was interested until he asked her to marry him.

Eric's choice may have been a surprise, but it was a good one. He and Florence had an unusually happy marriage. Within a few years, they had two little girls to take on bike rides through the old Chinese city of Tientsin or to the beaches of Pei-tai-ho.

But that happy time didn't last long. As the troubles in China grew worse, the London Missionary Society ran short of workers out in the villages. Could Eric go to work in the villages around Siaochang? He had spent the first few years of his life in that area, and his family was remembered and respected. His brother Rob, who had trained as a doctor, was taking over the hospital there.

At first, his answer was no. He was happy in Tientsin. His family was young, and he seemed ideally suited for his work at the college.

But over the next year the people of Siaochang were never far from his mind. Maybe a happy life in Tientsin wasn't what God intended for him. Maybe he should go to Siaochang, even if it meant leaving Florence and the children behind.

In 1937, he accepted the job.

Soon the London Missionary Society was receiving detailed reports of the devastation Eric encountered as he zigzagged across the vast plain on a wobbly bicycle. One day, he reported visiting an old man, a coffin maker, who was doing a good business. Hardly anyone

else was. Farms had been ruined by droughts and floods. The family
he was staying with that night had lost four members in the last year to
cholera. Village after village had been burned or bombed by the
Japanese. Not long ago, he had held a baptism in the middle of a
Japanese air raid.

But depressing as the conditions were, Eric loved his work. Here he
was *Li Mu Shi*—Pastor Liddell—living with the people, hearing their
problems, settling the disputes they brought to him. Especially he
loved the children. They laughed when he made coins and flowers
magically appear from their ears.

Siaochang was dangerous. The Japanese controlled the two main
railways, about 40 miles (60 kilometres) apart. In between, the Chinese
waged constant guerrilla war against the invaders. The missionaries
had to stay on the good side of all the armies, while dodging their
bullets and bombs.

One time, travelling by canal, Eric had to pass through first the
Japanese lines and then the guerrillas'. Not far from Siaochang,
a group of men with guns popped up on the river bank. The guerrillas
took Eric and his brother Rob to talk to their captain.

The Liddells' cook, who had insisted on coming along to look after
the two brothers, stayed with the barge and worried. Neither Japan
nor China was officially at war with Europe, so there was no reason
for the soldiers to kill missionaries. But the soldiers were young—only
16 or 17—and nervous, and an "accident" could easily happen.

The cook waited for over an hour, more and more sure that he
would never see his friends again and that he himself would be killed.

Suddenly he heard voices. It was Rob and Eric, talking and
laughing with the boys who only a short time before had been holding
them at gunpoint. The guerrilla captain turned out to be a graduate of
the mission school at Siaochang.

Many of the Japanese officers deliberately harassed the
missionaries, trying to get them to leave. Eric's natural diplomacy was
essential. He had to smuggle Chinese money from Tientsin through
the Japanese lines to pay the staff and buy supplies. Florence used to
hollow out a French loaf, stuff it full of money, then stick it upside
down in his knapsack. The Japanese would usually search the people
crossing their checkpoints. "But Eric would whip out his wallet and
show the soldiers pictures of his children," Florence recalls. "Most of
the soldiers were just farm kids conscripted into the army, and they

were desperately homesick. They'd get out pictures of their families too, and Eric would have them crying in no time. Then they'd pat him on the back and send him off."

Meanwhile, the war spread. With the Chinese Communists and Nationalists fighting among themselves, the Japanese were controlling more and more of the country.

Eric worried about Florence and their two daughters. They were certain that the Japanese would enter World War II—which would make the British into enemies. Missionaries might be imprisoned. They decided that Florence and the children should go to live with her parents in Canada. Eric would stay on for a while, hoping he could still be some help.

In May 1941, Florence set sail for Canada. It didn't occur to her that she might never see Eric again.

As 10-year-old David Michell stepped through the high, strong walls of the Japanese prison camp at Weihsien, he saw a strange crowd of people staring back at him. They were dressed in a weird assortment of clothes; their faces all showed marks of malnutrition and stress.

David had been taken prisoner at a school for missionaries' children. Japan had entered the war, and all "enemy nationals" were being interned.

That night, along with eight other boys, David laid his mattress down in a tiny basement room. As he lay in the dark he heard the crack of thunder and the sound of rain. Slowly water began to seep into the room. He tried not to think about it. Or about the plaster that kept dropping onto his bed. And the stink of the open sewers. And the scrabbling sound that he knew was rats. But most of all, he tried not to think about his family and whether he would ever see them again.

Compared to some of the other camps, Weihsien wasn't bad. No one was tortured or beaten. The Japanese let the prisoners run the camp their own way, as long as no one attempted to escape. The people of the camp divided up the chores—cooking, washing up, cleaning, gathering coal dust to make fuel; everyone did three hours of work a day.

Teachers from the various schools for missionaries' children continued to teach classes. There were regular church services and Bible groups and classes in every kind of subject—philosophy, religion, literature. There were even productions of plays and musical concerts.

Yet Weihsien had serious problems. More than 1,500 people—missionaries, businessmen, secretaries, prostitutes—were jammed into the space of three football fields. It was as if all the students in a big high school were forced to live in the school 24 hours a day. Space became precious.

So did food. The people of the camp suffered from malnutrition. This, along with the overflowing toilets, open cesspools and endless line-ups, sawed at the taut nerves of the prisoners. There was constant bickering and complaining.

With a few exceptions. David Michell noticed one man who always seemed to be smiling. Shortly after David arrived, another boy whispered to him, "That's Eric Liddell, the Olympic runner. The man who didn't run on Sunday."

In March 1943, Eric and all the British and Americans in Tientsin had been rounded up and sent to the camp at Weihsien.

David began to see a lot of this man. In the middle of all the misery, he always seemed to have a joke or a cheerful word. Twice a day all the people in the camp would gather to be counted by the Japanese guards to make sure that no one had escaped. As warden for the dormitories where David lived, Eric kept people in line and smoothed over problems with the guards. Although he had his own classes to teach, once a week he would take over from David's teachers, giving them a chance to relax. And every Sunday, there he was in the Bible class or the pulpit, usually speaking on his favourite passages, the Sermon on the Mount and St. Paul's words about love in I Corinthians 13.

And because he applied those passages to his own life, little by little Eric Liddell made a difference in the camp.

With some others, he started a sports program for young people. After a game, he could be seen binding the precious field hockey sticks with strips torn from his own sheets.

He even broke the rule that had made him famous. Once some of the teenagers decided to have a field hockey game on a Sunday. Because there was no one to referee, the game turned into a fight. Next Sunday Eric was there with his whistle, and the Sunday games went on.

As well as carrying a heavy teaching load, he was an active member of almost every camp committee. But much of his time was spent talking with people who were finding the strain of the camp too much to bear. Two men later said they were on the verge of suicide when Eric pulled them out of their depression. Another young man was completely disillusioned by the horrible conditions of the camp and the selfishness of the prisoners. Years later he wrote Florence about it. "He thought God had forgotten them—until he met Eric," she recalls.

He also did chores for the elderly and the sick. A woman who had been a prostitute was particularly grateful for his help. He was the only man, she said, who ever helped her without expecting something in return. And he never made her feel ashamed. When two patients at the point of death from typhoid were isolated in the ramshackle camp morgue, Eric visited them.

Young as he was, David Michell soon realized that there was a special strength in Eric Liddell. "In spite of the way everybody else cursed the Japanese, the conditions, the food, nobody ever heard Eric Liddell complain or say an unkind word. His faith was not shaken, no matter what happened. And that confidence in God spread from him to others."

Annie Buchan, the matron of the hospital in Siaochang where Eric had served as pastor and superintendent for several years, was the first to notice the change in Eric. When she arrived in Weihsien, she saw that he was slowing down. The old spring was gone from his step.

He confessed to her that he had been getting terrible headaches and feeling depressed.

As they sat together one day under the clump of trees by the camp hospital, she asked him how he was.

Eric smiled. "The doctors thought I might have had a stroke at first, but now they think I've had a nervous breakdown. They said I've been working too hard."

Annie tried to reassure him. "They're right about that," she said. Only a few days before, she had seen him carrying 50-pound (23-kilogram) Red Cross packages to help some of the elderly prisoners.

Eric frowned. "I've been through bad times before. It bothers me that I should break down now. I should have had more faith. I should have been able to cast it all on the Lord."

"Don't be too hard on yourself," Annie told him. "Have you heard from Flo?"

"Yes, just recently." Many in the camp didn't even know Eric had a family; he was too busy listening to everyone else's problems to talk about his own. But Annie knew how much he missed them. "I'm off to send her a letter now," he said.

The next day he was dead, at 43. The autopsy showed that he had had a brain tumour.

A s they trudged back through the wind and dust from the memorial service, the people of the camp thought about Eric's last words. Just before slipping into a coma, he said to Annie Buchan, "It's complete surrender." Strange words from a man who said he didn't like to be beaten. Had he finally been defeated by his illness and the hard life of the prison camp?

Unlike Elizabeth Fry or William Wilberforce, Eric Liddell did not make any great changes. No one would say that modern China is different today because of him. It was not so much what he did that was important, it was what he was.

In many ways he was a very ordinary man. That was the mystery about Eric Liddell: a runner inexperienced in the 400 metres who became an Olympic champion; a poor public speaker who converted hundreds of people; a retiring man who was popular everywhere he went. As they went about the endless dreary round of chores over the next few days, Eric's friends began to realize the truth about him. He was in fact a very ordinary man. But he had become extraordinary because he gave his life to God. He had surrendered not to the hardships and pressures of life, but to Christ.

Once, on a trip back to Scotland, Eric had told an audience, "We are all missionaries. We carry our religion with us.... Wherever we go, we either bring people nearer to Christ, or we repel them from Christ."

Eric Liddell followed his own advice.

When she heard that her husband had died, Florence Liddell's first thought was to throw herself off a bridge. "Eric had always been miles ahead of me spiritually," she says. "But all of a sudden, I felt this faith welling up inside me." Eric had passed his faith on to her, and it has helped her ever since.

In her home in a big white farmhouse near Hamilton, Ontario, she keeps a thick file of letters from people all over the world who knew or were inspired by her husband.

David Michell was reunited with his parents. But he remembered the man who had been his hero: "If being a Christian meant being like Eric Liddell, then I wanted to be a Christian!" As a high school student, he began to tell others about him. Eventually Michell himself was ordained and became the Canadian director of the Overseas Missionary Fellowship, an organization that sends missionaries to the Orient.

And 37 years after Eric Liddell's death, a 13-year-old boy watched the movie *Chariots of Fire,* the story of Eric Liddell and the 1924 Olympics. "Mom," he said quietly as they left the theatre, "I think that guy's my hero."

His mother looked surprised. "But you're always telling me that Superman's your hero."

The boy shook his head. "That's different. Superman's plastic. This guy's for real."

BOB McCLURE

Adventure equals risk plus a purpose

BOB McCLURE

Why did you do it?''

The question came at the end of another television interview with Bob McClure, medical missionary, former head of the United Church of Canada and now, in his seventies, a media star. In his 50 years working all over the world as a surgeon, he'd also been a mechanic for the Red Cross, a bomb demolition expert and even a blood donor for his own operations.

If the interviewer expected a pious answer when he asked McClure why he'd led such a remarkable life, he didn't get it.

With his usual explosive energy, McClure leaned toward the camera and almost shouted: "I did it because it was so much *fun!*"

Early in his career as a missionary, Bob McClure decided on a formula for his life: A = r + p. *Adventure* equals *risk* plus a *purpose*. He loved going to new places, meeting new people, trying new things. It·didn't seem to bother him if there were a few bullets flying around, as long as there was a good reason for taking the risk.

That was where his religion came in. Bob McClure was no mystic. He never heard any voices in the night. But he believed that God

had given him a generous share of talent and expected him to use it. So
when he was only 13 he decided to follow the example of his father
and become a doctor and a missionary.

Like Eric Liddell, Bob McClure spent much of his early life in
China and returned to serve there after going to university back home.
During the twenties and thirties he was stationed in Honan, in North
China. But when the Japanese advanced, the Christian missionaries
were forced to leave Honan. Most tried to help out in other parts of
China.

So in January 1939, Bob McClure found himself on the world's
longest official secret: the Burma Road. Realizing that the Japanese
would eventually control the coast of China, Chinese leaders ordered
a huge road to be built from Southeast Asia through the mountain
ranges separating Burma and China. The Chinese portion of the road
was built by hand, and it was said that if all the people who had died
building it were laid end to end, they would line both sides of the 700-
mile (1,125-kilometre) section. As Bob McClure struggled up mountain
passes as high as 9,500 feet (3,000 metres), he remembered the warning
of a colleague that travelling on the Burma Road would be "like an
ant climbing over corrugated iron."

The road became an essential artery during World War II in the
work of the Red Cross, the Friends' Ambulance Unit and other war
relief organizations. Their help was desperately needed. But medical
workers were useless if they didn't have supplies to work with. The
relief organizations needed trucks to bring in instruments, drugs and
bandages and to distribute them to medical stations in Free China that
were served by the Burma Road.

The obvious man to organize the fleet was Bob McClure. Not only
could he sew a wound up in record time while bombs crashed about
him, but he was a talented mechanic. So along with his medical work,
McClure began to handle the importing of medical supplies and the
trucks to carry them.

Once they arrived, the trucks had to be driven into China, through
the Japanese air raids. "We thought at first that the Japanese would
respect the Red Cross," recalls McClure, "but we early found out that
we were wrong."

McClure and his team would dash along the ramshackle road
through the night, trying to get as far as possible into China before

dawn and the air raids. If they were lucky, they could cover a hundred miles (160 kilometres), with no breakdowns, before they had to stop and camouflage the trucks, hiding beneath a tree or in a ditch and disguising the trucks with hay.

"The airplanes would sometimes come so low that you could see the pilot and he could see you," says McClure. Often the drivers huddled under the hay covering one truck would see another truck go up in flames. Sometimes their own trucks would be hit. But the Japanese pilots always missed the gasoline tanks, and the fleet never lost a man.

McClure quickly learned the best hiding spots. Grave mounds were his favourite, for no bullet could pierce a tombstone. Once during an air raid he and an American soldier both dived for what they thought was a grave mound. They quickly discovered it was a manure heap.

Most of the vehicles were driven in from their port of arrival, but one took a different route. At a fund-raising lunch during a trip home to North America, McClure noticed that the chairman of the

lunch hadn't contributed anything. McClure suggested he should have
a project of his own—an ambulance truck. The judge agreed—on
condition that the ambulance be named the *Mary O'Connor* after his
wife. Four months later the judge got a cable from China. The *Mary
O'Connor* had been blown apart by the Japanese during the British
forces' retreat from Burma. The judge was furious and decided to
replace the ambulance immediately. But by now the Japanese had captured most of Southeast Asia. There was no port where the ambulance
could be landed and driven in. McClure had the ambulance sent to India, where it was broken down into its smallest parts and then flown
into China by parcel post. There McClure reassembled it. This time
the *Mary O'Connor* lasted until the end of the war.

With the Japanese controlling the coast, the air route from
India over the Himalayas was now the only way into China. It was full
of "stuffed clouds"—stuffed with granite! Without sophisticated
radar equipment, the pilots often got lost in the mountains, winding
through the valleys until they ran out of fuel. Others crashed onto the
mountains. Many pilots died of injuries or were lost and died of
exhaustion.

McClure and his colleagues thought of a solution for this waste of
good young men. First they needed the cooperation of the local tribespeople. Each tribe lived in its own valley, almost entirely cut off from
the world. McClure and his medical team began to penetrate these
valleys. There they found many people who needed medical
help—especially children. The doctors would take a child back to the
base camp and repair the damage. In return, that child and his family
became their representatives in the village, in charge of making sure
that downed airmen were rescued and handed over to the Americans.

One young patient named Jimmy had broken his leg four years
earlier, and it had never properly healed. It took a year and numerous
operations before his leg was repaired. Meanwhile, Jimmy encouraged
soldiers who were depressed about their injuries. "I've been operated
on four times," he would scold them, showing his scars. "What's the
matter with you? This is nothing. The doctors here can do anything
for you."

Jimmy was good for morale, but eventually he went home. And it was in his valley that the first airman was rescued, a young Canadian who had been accompanying Lord Mountbatten on a secret mission over China.

Sometimes a flier would be too severely injured to make his way to a village. The solution was to send the doctor to him. There was only one doctor on the team who not only spoke Chinese and knew the area, but was also trained in parachute jumping.... McClure soon found himself leaping from planes into the mountainous valleys. After tending his patient he would scramble down to the nearest village to get help to carry the man out. By walkie-talkie he would keep the American forces informed of their whereabouts. The Americans would meet them along the Burma Road, with payment for the guides.

Since the Japanese had cut off the villagers' supply of salt, the Americans rewarded them with salt. They would get each rescued man's weight in salt—twice his weight if he had to be carried out.

The Japanese also offered a reward for captured airmen: enough gold to support an entire village for life. Not once did a tribesman take them up on their offer.

The rescue missions were dangerous, but then so was surgery. The hospitals were as close as possible to the front, so that the wounded could be treated quickly. McClure and his team might set up an operating room on the front porch of a temple, draping it with parachute silk to keep out the dust and flies. Here they would perform six or more operations a day. In the operating room, McClure demanded complete dedication. His staff nicknamed him "General McCurdle" for his blood-curdling rages whenever someone slipped up.

Often medical stations were disguised to look like harmless hillside villages, complete with animals wandering around. But there was always the danger the bombers would discover the deception. One day, McClure was sure the village had been found. In the middle of an operation, the room began to shake and the ceiling started to fall in. McClure glanced up, only to see that a water buffalo had fallen down a slope onto the building.

Another time the "village" *was* bombed, and the corner of the operating room blown off. McClure and his colleagues kept right on with the operation.

Wounds were not the only problem. During the rainy season, as many as 70 percent of the Chinese troops could be out of action with various diseases—cholera, typhus fever and malaria. And as the Japanese began to retreat, McClure noticed another problem. In the reclaimed cities, large numbers of children were being brought in with missing hands and burned faces. Others never made it to the hospital. They had been playing with unexploded grenades and bombs. McClure decided to try some preventive medicine. From American engineers the doctor learned how to deal with explosives. When he wasn't in the hospital, he was running about the city, searching for unexploded bombs.

Despite all the risks, the medical staff found there was little time to think about danger. McClure developed the attitude that "God keeps us as long as he wants to use us, and when our time's up it doesn't make much difference where we are, in how safe a spot, we're due to be taken."

But the work was also satisfying. They knew they were doing something the Chinese people couldn't yet do for themselves. Between emergencies they held classes for Chinese medical practitioners, so that the Chinese could carry on more of the work themselves.

At the end of one of the sessions, a Chinese student began a long harangue. We haven't really heard anything we didn't already know, he told his fellow students. McClure braced himself for criticism. Instead the student said, "You know as well as I that what we need is the spirit of these teachers of ours who are Christians."

The spirit of service, along with many other programs begun by medical missionaries, would continue after the war. But McClure wouldn't be there to see it. He had been called home to deal with a family emergency. By the time he was ready to return to China, the Communists had taken over the country's government. McClure was considered a friend of Generalissimo Chiang Kai-Shek, the former ruler. He was on the Chinese Communists' "wanted" list. It would be

30 years before McClure could return to the country where he had spent most of his life.

He was deeply disappointed. "But by now," he says, "I had developed enough faith to know that if God closes one door he opens another."

McClure resigned himself to the idea that he would probably never go back to China. Yet adventure was far from over in his life. Although his bomb-dodging days were done, he would have the fun of learning about other societies and taking on the challenging jobs that no one else would do.

At first, he joined a medical clinic in Toronto, Canada, and set out to enjoy the family he had scarcely seen in the last 12 years: his wife Amy, three daughters, and a son. But he found he was doing only as many operations in a month as he used to do in a day. If God really wanted to use his talents fully, this certainly wasn't the place.

Then in the summer of 1950 a restless and frustrated McClure heard from a friend that there was a job for a surgeon at a missionary hospital in the Gaza Strip. Gaza was only a small strip of land just south of Israel, but it was choked with refugees who had fled Palestine during the Arab-Israeli War of 1948. As chief of surgery, McClure would be serving not only the local residents, but 125,000 people living in a city of tents.

McClure was delighted to be back at work, serving people who really needed help, doing a job few others would take on and not being very well paid for it. The hospital staff and local people soon grew used to the sight of the Canadian doctor racing about the countryside on his bike or charging out of a successful operation in blood-spattered undershirt and shorts, bellowing for his indispensible iced tea.

As in China, McClure's ultimate aim was to make sure that he and other missionaries were no longer needed. Gathering the brightest hospital helpers around him, he began to transform them into skilled anaesthetists and medical technicians. With funds from private donors in Canada, he bought X-ray equipment and began a fight against tuberculosis.

But while McClure was serving the people of Gaza, he was also learning from them. As he studied Arabic, he found that Muslim Arabs constantly referred to God. Everything was followed by *Inshallah*—"If Allah wills." Was this just habit, or were they really constantly aware of God's presence in their lives?

Some time later, he found himself on a train full of soldiers. The train was going to stop only a few minutes for lunch, and McClure knew his only chance of getting anything from the snackbar was to be the first there. As the train slowed, McClure leaped from the car and dashed to the tiny snackbar. No one followed him. When he looked back he saw that all the soldiers had removed their shoes and were saying their noon prayers instead of eating.

On another occasion, a leader from a refugee camp came to have a broken kneecap repaired. The sheik, who had never had an operation before and didn't think much of the loud-talking Christian missionary, was worried and tense as he was rolled into the operating room. Then, as was his habit before the first operation of every day, McClure bowed and prayed aloud: "Allah, grant us your blessing when we do our work this day and grant that we may try to do our work in the spirit in which Jesus Christ healed people in his time." The sheik fell quietly asleep.

Several weeks later, when McClure was removing the cast, the sheik thanked him for the prayer. Then the sheik asked, "Why is it that you only pray before the first operation? That is not enough, my friend. All patients are frightened. Raise your hand and promise that from now on you will pray before every operation."

McClure kept the promise.

G aza was only a four-year stop on the way to another job, as chief surgeon at a United Church mission hospital at Ratlam in central India. Here again McClure would learn a lesson in faith from the local people.

Through the Ratlam Rotary Club, McClure met a former follower of Mahatma Gandhi in the movement for the independence of India. Manohar Nagpal had joined in the mass demonstrations against the British government. The demonstrators were totally non-violent. They would not beat away the police dogs nor curse the policemen who were only doing their jobs. Nagpal was sentenced four times to mandatory terms of "two-years-less-one-day" for "civil disobedience" by a reluctant judge but was released halfway through the last term after India gained independence. Nagpal regularly sent Christmas cards and letters to the British judge who had sentenced him. He summed up the pacifists' attitude for McClure: "We had to learn to hate the British government and to love every individual Englishman."

At times McClure felt that our so-called Christian society in the Western world suffered by comparison with the attitudes of some of his Indian friends.

Yet there were other attitudes in India that disturbed him, that showed him that as a Christian he had something to offer the people of Ratlam. "In India you saw great poverty," he recalls, "and you saw people who had lots of everything and were not ready to share it, except with their own little clique." When McClure suggested that the Rotary Club start an orphanage, his friend Nagpal explained that it wouldn't work; Muslim overseers couldn't be trusted to treat Hindu children well and vice versa.

With his startlingly practical approach to Christianity, McClure began to demonstrate to friends in Ratlam the Christian belief in the importance of each person and our duty to give real help to that person.

Once, he was in the middle of a serious operation when it was discovered that the blood donor for the operation, the patient's husband, had fled. McClure jumped up on the donor's table himself and supplied the necessary blood.

Another time he was travelling to a Rotary meeting with some friends when they met a beggar with a bad leg. Each of McClure's friends gave him a coin. McClure didn't give him anything. Instead he told the beggar to come to the hospital so that his leg could be made better.

He believes his own work and that of other missionaries have had an effect. The beggar now has a job, through the Rotary Club, making tricycles for paraplegics. Indians are carrying on the work of public health—one of McClure's favourite projects—recognizing that individual health isn't enough; the only way to protect yourself from disease is to make sure that your neighbour is healthy as well. McClure regularly visits Ratlam and he feels "terrifically optimistic" about the changing attitudes in India. Christianity is not coming to India in a great wave of conversions, he says, "but very quietly, just like Jesus said, with a little change here, a little change there...."

After 13 years in India, at the age of 67, McClure returned to Canada in 1968. There he spent two and a half years as Moderator of the United Church, outraging and delighting Canadians with his unusual opinions on everything from church offerings to teenage sex.

No one really believed that McClure would retire. He didn't. In December 1971 he and his wife, Amy, went to the American Methodist Hospital in Sarawak, on the island of Borneo in Southeast Asia. McClure was pleased to discover that many of the nurses there spoke Mandarin Chinese. It was even better to find that he had not lost any of his surgical skills.

He would need them. Shortly after the McClures arrived, the chief surgeon went on leave. There was no one to replace him. At 72, McClure found himself the only doctor at the hospital. In one month, he did 30 major and 79 minor operations, more than had ever been done when there were two doctors at the hospital.

Finally, after eight months, help came in the form of a Malaysian doctor. McClure quickly recovered his energy, which he then threw into organizing a public health program for the Iban, the former headhunters who lived along the Rajang River in communal longhouses built on stilts. McClure organized medical teams to visit the Iban villages to encourage better nutrition and sewage systems, inoculate them against disease and help with family planning.

McClure liked what he discovered about the Iban. They had one of the most peaceful, sensible societies he had ever encountered, and they knew how to look after one another. Once McClure asked a patient who was looking after her children while she was in hospital. "What a fool of a question!" she exclaimed. "My neighbour's looking after them, of course." The patient was shocked when McClure asked if she was paying her neighbour. But when her neighbour came to the hospital for an operation next month, naturally she would look after her neighbour's children.

With several families sharing one "longhouse," the Iban had to develop great self-control. Children were not even allowed to wrestle for fear they would lose their tempers. At 10, each child was given a machete knife, which he wore at all times to hunt, cut food and defend himself against cobras. Yet though every Iban carried a machete, in his two years at the hospital McClure never saw a knife wound made in anger. "There is absolutely no violence in those communities," he says. "You never even hear anyone raise his voice."

There wasn't any stealing among the Iban, either. They seemed to be happy with what they had, rather than always craving more things. On one wet trip up the river, an Iban woman admired McClure's watch and asked if it was waterproof. McClure replied that it was. The woman thought for a moment, then said that she preferred to tell the time by the sun. "It's self-winding too," she smiled.

On another occasion, McClure left his camera behind in a hired boat. He had given up any hope of seeing his camera again, when a boatman turned up with it. The boatman apologized for being so long—it had taken him three days to find McClure. He wouldn't dream of accepting a reward. But he shyly asked if the doctor might lend him the camera some day to take a picture.

I f McClure admired the Iban, he also admired the missionaries who had worked in Sarawak. Rather than trying to transplant Western values and complicated religious ideas into Borneo, they had given the Iban the basic Christian message and left them to apply it to their own way of life. "This is the juice of Christian missions today," McClure emphasizes. "We don't want to make the Muslims or the Hindus just like us. We want to add a Christian flavour to their cultures."

After Sarawak, McClure went on brief stints to South America and the West Indies and Africa. As a doctor, he has finally retired. But he's still a missionary. At countless speaking engagements across Canada he passes on the lessons he's learned from people around the world and criticizes the failings of Western society.

"There's no society on earth that can't teach us something," he declares.

Now in his eighties and looking at least 15 years younger, he still bounces around the world, visiting old friends and reporting on development projects. And he's still having fun.

MOTHER TERESA

Bringing hope to the nightmare city

MOTHER TERESA

The girls had prepared a special ceremony to say good-bye to their principal. There were songs and tears and shared memories of the 19 years that Mother had taught in the Loreto convent school in Calcutta.

Then came the moment when the huge door closed behind her, shutting her off from the comfort and security of the convent. At the age of 37 she stood alone in what one Indian prime minister had called "the nightmare city." She had nothing but 60 cents in her pocket and the belief that God had called her to serve the poorest of the poor.

Early in this century, a group of Yugoslav priests went to work as missionaries in India. Their letters home were often read aloud by the local priests. One person who listened with special interest was Agnes Gonxha Bojaxha, the daughter of an Albanian shopkeeper. Since the age of 12 she had felt she should become a nun. Because of those inspiring letters, she decided she wanted to serve in India.

In 1928, at the age of 18, she joined the Loreto order. A year later, she was sent to Calcutta, in the northeast corner of India.

Calcutta must have been a shock for the young nun, with its huge decaying mansions invaded by swarms of squatters, its piles of steaming garbage, its open sewers and endless slums. For the poor who were lucky, there were shacks of earth and bamboo. For the less fortunate, there were the streets. Wealthier people stepped over homeless adults and children sleeping on the sidewalks. Close to a million people were born, lived and died on the streets of the city, without permanent homes of any kind.

The convent of the Loreto order was an oasis in this vast desert of despair. Blocked off from the surrounding slums by high walls, the convent provided a residence for the nuns, a chapel and a school, St. Mary's, attended by daughters of Calcutta's wealthy families. Here, amid beautiful gardens and peaceful, yellow-washed walls, Agnes, now known as Teresa, taught for 19 years.

Mother Teresa was popular with her young students. At St. Mary's, she was moulding the future mothers, doctors and teachers that India so badly needed. She hoped that some might hear the call, as she had, and become nuns.

But there were times when, looking from her window over the roofs of the slums, she wondered if this was what God had brought her to India for. When her students visited the slums and hospitals on weekends, they came back with distressing stories of poverty and disease. She herself had seen leprosy victims begging, children starving, and bundles of rags, lying on the sidewalks, that turned out to be human beings. Was there something more that God wanted her to do?

Mother Teresa got her answer on September 10, 1946. On a crowded train, she heard "a call within a call."

"The message was quite clear," she later explained to a friend. "I was to leave the convent and help the poor while living among them. It was an order."

It took two years to get permission to leave the convent. But finally, in 1948, she began her new life. On her final day, Mother Teresa found that it was hard to obey God: "To leave Loreto was my greatest sacrifice, the most difficult thing I have ever done. It was much more difficult than to leave my family to enter religious life. Loreto meant everything to me." Her students from St. Mary's sang for her, many of them with tears streaming down their cheeks. Then the door of the convent closed, and she was alone.

She decided to begin with what she knew best: teaching. Finding a clearing in the garbage of a public park, she gathered a small group of children and began teaching them the alphabet and how to keep themselves clean. She visited the poor in their homes, listening to their troubles, bringing them whatever food and medical help she could. Having no money of her own, she begged when necessary, gave away all she received and trusted in God.

It was a difficult and lonely time. She wrote in her diary: "Today I learned a good lesson. The poverty of the poor must be so hard for them. While looking for a home, I walked and walked till my arms and legs ached. I thought how much they must ache in body and soul looking for a home, food and health. Then the comfort of Loreto came to tempt me. But of free choice, my God, and out of love for You, I desire to remain and do whatever be Your holy will in my regard. Give me courage now, this moment."

Mother Teresa was looking for a home not only for herself, but for the other women she hoped would join her. A few months after she left the convent, a wealthy Christian family offered her the top floor of their mansion. One night, she heard a knock at the door of the flat. When she opened it, there stood a familiar, frail figure, even smaller than herself. "Mother, I have come to join you," said one of her students from Loreto.

Together they shared the hard life of serving the poor. Soon other girls from Loreto joined them, 10 in all. They worked long hours with no luxuries of any kind. Mother Teresa explained to her followers that in order to truly serve the poor they must live like the poor. And so the sisters dressed in coarse cotton saris, ate plain food and lived in simple unadorned dormitories.

They rose at 4:00 in the morning and prayed until 6:30, when they ate breakfast, did the laundry and cleaned the house. Then they went out to work, always travelling in twos.

It was a daunting task for young girls, many of them from wealthy families. They had to tend the loathsome sores of people whose fingers and feet had been rotted away by leprosy. Sometimes they had to beg for money, food or medicine. But Mother Teresa inspired them with her own courage and the passage from Matthew 25 that has been the basis of all her work:

*"...for I was hungry and you gave me food, I was thirsty
and you gave me drink. I was a stranger and you welcomed
me, I was naked and you clothed me, I was sick and you
visited me, I was in prison and you came to me.... Truly,
I say to you, as you did it to one of the least of these my
brethren, you did it to me."*

In every person they met, Mother Teresa explained, they should see
Christ, even if he was in a "distressing disguise."

Those who wore the most distressing disguise of all were the hundreds who died on the streets every year, alone and uncared for, their bodies often hideously disfigured. One day, Mother Teresa found a woman lying outside a hospital, half-eaten by rats and cockroaches. Mother Teresa carried the women into the hospital, but the staff would not accept her; they had enough trouble looking after patients who had a chance of recovering. They only gave in when the determined nun refused to leave.

This happened to Mother Teresa several times. Finally she cried, "Cats and dogs are treated better than this," and marched off to the officials of Calcutta to ask for a home where the sisters could look after the dying.

In 1952 Nirmal Hriday, the Place of the Pure Heart, opened. The spot chosen was ideal in one way. It was a former hostel for Hindu pilgrims, near the Kalighat temple where devout Hindus came to burn their dead. The sisters would find many in need, for any Hindu who knew he was dying would try to reach Kalighat.

But many local people feared that the sisters would try to convert the dying. Four hundred Hindu priests demonstrated angrily against the opening of a Catholic institution within the temple grounds. Mother Teresa answered only by saying, "If you want to kill me, kill me. But do not disturb the inmates. Let them die in peace." The demonstration ended.

Others complained to the police commissioner, who promised to remove the sisters. But first, he had to see the place for himself. On the day of his visit, Mother Teresa was there, tending to a patient. Maggots were crawling from the patient's sores, and the stench from his body was terrible. When the police commissioner emerged from the building, he told the men who had complained, "I have given my word that I would push this lady out and I will keep it. But before I do, you must get your mothers and your sisters to do the work she is doing. Only then will I exercise my authority." No one volunteered.

Shortly after, one of the priests from the Kali temple, suffering horribly from cholera, was rescued from the streets by the sisters. He died peacefully in the luminous quiet of Nirmal Hriday.

Today the priests and local people see the sisters not as enemies but as friends in the service of God; some even think of Mother Teresa as the incarnation of the goddess Kali.

No one tries to convert the Hindus and Muslims who come to die at Nirmal Hriday. All are allowed to die and be buried or cremated according to their beliefs. The purpose in serving the dying, says Mother Teresa, is "that they too may know that they are the children of God and that they are not forgotten and that they are loved and cared about."

The sisters bring peace to the last moments of their patients. "I have lived like an animal on the streets," said one old man to Mother Teresa, "but I'm going to die like an angel."

From the care of the dying, Mother Teresa's newly formed order, the Missionaries of Charity, turned to the care of those who had just been born. Because women who had children before they were married were rejected by their families and neighbours, many abandoned their babies, leaving them on the streets or in garbage cans. Older children, orphaned or deserted, wandered the streets. To look after these children, the sisters acquired another house, Shishu Bhavan. It also became a centre for giving food and medicine to the poor.

One day in 1957, a new challenge arrived at Shishu Bhavan: five men with leprosy who had been fired from their jobs and could find no shelter or food. They begged Mother Teresa to take them in. And since it is her policy never to turn anyone away, she gave them the shelter they needed.

Half the world's 15 million leprosy sufferers live in India. The Missionaries realized that, like the dying and the abandoned children, the leprosy victims did not just suffer in their bodies; they also suffered because no one wanted them. So great is the terror of leprosy that anyone who contracts it, no matter how important, is rejected by his family and neighbours. One high-ranking government official explained: "After I got the disease, I withdrew from society. I withdrew so much I reached a stage where I had nobody who wanted or cared for me but the Missionaries of Charity."

The sisters decided that it was time to help the sufferers. At first they had difficulty starting dispensaries. When a local politician objected to having permanent treatment centres close to his home, the sisters were forced to treat their patients from trucks that travelled around the slums. As often happened, what looked like a problem turned out to be an improvement. "Bless you, councillor," Mother Teresa said to the politician. "You have increased our efficiency ten times."

Later the government donated 34 acres outside of Calcutta for the missionaries to start the first of many communities for leprosy patients. At Shantinagar, the Place of Peace, they learn to support themselves and to treat their own disease. With modern medicines, many are now being cured.

One of Mother Teresa's frustrations was that the Church would not allow her to start any centres outside Calcutta until ten years after her order was founded. But as soon as the ten years was up, the sisters began spreading their work through India and then around the world—to Venezuela, Australia, Jordan, Rome, New York and even to Yemen, where no Christian had worshipped for 600 years.

Mother Teresa saw that there were many areas where it would be useful to have male helpers and priests to perform the sacraments. She encouraged the founding of a companion organization, the Missionary Brothers of Charity.

Meanwhile, many people around the world wanted to help the sisters in their work. So in 1969 the International Association of Co-workers of Mother Teresa was started. The Co-workers raise money and supplies for Mother Teresa's projects around the world and also serve in their own communities. In Western countries, of course, people are rarely as poor as the slum-dwellers of Calcutta. But even in the wealthiest countries, Mother Teresa says, "you have a different kind of poverty—a poverty of the spirit, of loneliness and of being unwanted.''

The sisters still face enormous problems. Yet they have made a difference in the lives of thousands of people. Mother Teresa gives all the credit to God: ''Humanly speaking [our success] is impossible, out of the question. Because none of us has got the experience. None of us has got the things that the world looks for. This is the miracle of all those little Sisters around the world. God is using them—they are just little instruments in His hands. But they have their conviction. As long as any of us has this conviction we are all right. The work will prosper.''

Mother Teresa never worries about where the money for her many expensive projects will come from. ''I never think of it,'' she says. ''It always comes. The Lord sends it. We do His work; He provides the means. If He does not give us the means, that shows He does not want the work. So why worry?''

God also sends helpers. One Indian student describes how he was on his way to meet his friends to see a movie, when a woman in a white sari beckoned to him. He realized later it was Mother Teresa herself. ''The nun wanted my help to pick up a half-dead man sprawled over a garbage heap. I was simply horrified. The man's body was decomposing and emitting a foul stench. But the nun's face appealed to me as no one's had ever done before. Almost in a trance I found myself helping her. Something made me jump into the ambulance and go with them to their home. There I went down on my knees and helped to wash the dying man's sore-covered feet. I felt that this was the first worthwhile act that I had ever done in my whole life.''

Another volunteer says simply, ''She makes you want to climb mountains for her.''

Mother Teresa is not perfect. She is not always right. Her followers and patrons have often disagreed with her, but they have never lost respect for her. She is also blessed with an energy that would be extraordinary in a girl, let alone a frail woman now in her seventies.

A young Canadian woman who worked for six months with the Missionaries of Charity explained how Mother Teresa keeps going amid such vast problems: "She is able to see individuals, rather than large groups of people. She deals with the person that Christ has set before her at that moment—and then the next person and then the next. She is acutely aware of each person she meets; you know that when she's talking to you, you have 100 percent of her attention.

"Yet, at the same time, she notices so much more than you or I would. One time at the Home for the Dying she tapped my arm. I hadn't even realized that she'd come in. And she said to me, 'That man over there needs water.' I'd been working there all morning, yet I hadn't noticed."

Mother Teresa shows the same consideration for the sisters, who she says "are my strength." When the sisters go to bed at nine o'clock, Mother Teresa begins her clerical work, answering letters from around the world well into the night.

"The sisters told me," the Canadian continued, "that they often found her asleep in the hall on the stone floor, because she didn't want to come in and wake anybody up."

On another occasion, Mother Teresa and five sisters arrived in Melbourne, Australia, and found a neglected house as a centre for their work. After cleaning the house, they retired for the night. Since Mother Teresa had broken her arm, the sisters piled blankets on one side of the bed so that she could sleep in comfort. The next morning, they awoke to find that the blankets had been spread over each of them to keep them warm during the cold night.

I f you asked Mother Teresa about these stories, she would ignore your questions. She never likes to speak of herself. Instead she would tell you about the dedicated work of her followers or about the lessons in love that she learns daily from the poor.

"I believe we need the poor as much as they need us," she insists. "We are the better for being in contact with them."

As an example, she often tells a story about a large family that had not eaten for several days. As soon as she heard of them, Mother Teresa took them some rice. The mother of the family immediately divided the rice into two portions and took half to the family next door. When Mother Teresa asked why she had done this, the woman explained that the other family also had not eaten for several days. "This is living love," says Mother Teresa. "It didn't matter to her that they were Muslims and she was a Hindu and it was given by a Christian sister. She knew that those people needed her love and they were her people."

The sun poured down on Varsity Stadium in Toronto. Hundreds of umbrellas sprang up like colourful mushrooms to protect the crowd. I sat on the grass, as close to the stage as possible, with four teenagers I had met just that morning.

We had been waiting five hours for the start of a peace rally organized by the Toronto Catholic Youth Corps. But what we had really come for was to see Mother Teresa. She would arrive from Winnipeg, speak to us briefly, then fly on to New York.

For all of the characters in this book, the early triumphs have been followed by trial and even personal tragedy. Francis of Assisi saw some of his original ideas distorted, even as his movement grew. Father Damien contracted leprosy. Eric Liddell died struggling with his own faith, tortured by an illness he didn't even know he had.

For Mother Teresa, perhaps the greatest trial has been the publicity that has grown around her work. It has brought her money and volunteers. But her fame is a trial, partly because she is shy, and so facing the huge crowds and staring cameras is difficult. Publicity embarrasses her because it focuses on her, proclaiming her a saint while she is still alive. She doesn't like to take credit for what she feels is God's work.

Mother Teresa believes that it is not she who is important but the people who work with her, the poor who suffer and the love of God that shines through them all. When she was told in 1979 that she had been awarded the Nobel Peace Prize, she said that she herself was not worthy but that she accepted "in the name of the poor."

When he was looking for stories about Mother Teresa's past, journalist Desmond Doig questioned the nuns who were still living in the Loreto convent. One young nun told him, "The remarkable thing about Mother Teresa was that she was ordinary.''

Mother Teresa would agree. Like all of the others in this book, she believes that she is a very ordinary person. What is special about her is that she allows God to work through her. She believes that all who love God can work for God's kingdom.

That hot day in Toronto, she spoke to us not of treaties between nations or declarations by the United Nations, but of how each of us can work for peace by acting with love toward each other. "If we stop thinking about what other people should do and start thinking about what each of us should do—you, I, all of us—starting today, little by little, we shall overcome.''

Along with St. Francis, William Wilberforce, Elizabeth Fry, Father Damien, Mary Slessor, Harriet Tubman, Dietrich Bonhoeffer, Eric Liddell and Bob McClure, Mother Teresa speaks to each of us when she says, ''Do not wait for leaders; do it alone, person to person.''